UNMAKING Marchant

ELLA JAMES

Unmaking Marchant
A Love, Inc. Series Novel
Copyright © 2014 by Ella James

ISBN-13: 978-0-9895084-2-1

Printed in the United States of America

Find out more about the author and upcoming books online at **www.ellajamesbooks.com** or friend her on Facebook at **www.facebook.com/ellajamesbooks**

SEE WHAT OTHERS ARE SAYING ABOUT

UNMAKING *Marchant*

BY ELLA JAMES

"This series/Author never disappoint! A rich Romance, a little darkness, and #SexyTimes that will make you blush."
- *Michelle @ The Passionate Bookworms*

"Ella James is on my top 20 top authors list. She has been since I found Selling Scarlett and the Love Inc. series just keeps getting better and better."
- *Jacki@Bout-A-BookBlog*

"I have read all of Ella James' book and I can honestly say that this is by far my favorite. I absolutely love that the story line of Lizzy/ Hunter continues and it picks up Adam from Taming Cross. I didn't like Marchant in Selling Scarlet nor Taming Cross, but I I found myself falling for him."
- *Sassyintx*

"Another novel in the Love Inc. series? Yes, please! I devoured Selling Scarlett and Taming Cross by this extremely talented author so I was chomping at the bit for this highly anticipated release. Unmaking Marchant had high expectations to reach, which it accomplished effortlessly."
- *H BestSellersBestStellars "HWR"*

"A little dark, a whole lot sexy and a book that will draw you in from the first chapter."
- *Pamela Sims*

PROLOGUE

Marchant

NEW ORLEANS, LOUISIANA
SATURDAY, MARCH 17, 2007

THE CASKET IS gold. The color of the sun. The color of Marissa's long, straight hair. I have the urge to open its lid, but that would be pointless. There's nothing inside. Because there's nothing left.

It's my fault. I know that just as surely as I know my goddamned name, even though I didn't kill her with my own two hands. I look down at them. They're bloody hands. Blood is seeping from the broken knuckles.

Wonder how long before the cops catch up with me.

I run a fingertip over the lid of the sunshine casket. The crimson smear gleams in the lamplight like something precious. And all of a sudden, I want to see more of it. So much more of it.

I look around the small mortuary viewing room for something sharp. My hands are shaking with the need for it—the need to end it all right now. I could do it. The funeral director is in his office. I can hear him pecking on a keyboard.

I could do it right now. No one would know.

I'm in the perfect place for death, after all—and I deserve to

1

die. Just ask Marissa.

I turn around slowly and stare at the floor-to-ceiling book-shelves on the left side of the room. So many books, and all the books so pointless. Like the casket, everything is pointless. Has always been pointless. Will always be pointless.

I try to push past the fuzziness inside my mind and think. Maybe I could use the glass on a frame to cut my wrists. I could even find the room where they embalm the bodies and use one of the knives. Whatever the way, I like the thought of dying here.

Right then, as if the gods ordain my thoughts, a letter open-er pops out at me from among the books and trinkets. It's long and brassy, pointed at the tip just like a dagger. It's resting near the bottom of the bookshelf, right in front of a staunch, burgundy hardback called *RESPECTING LIFE*.

Even in my current state, I can appreciate the irony.

I step across the foot-worn rug and lift the cool brass gently off of its perch. I'm looking down at it, thinking how much duller it looks than the ones they use in movies to stab the vil-lain, when the pecking stops.

The sweaty hair on the back of my neck tingles, like I just did a line of coke.

A second later, the double-doors burst open, and the cops pour in.

CHAPTER ONE

Suri

NAPA, CALIFORNIA
FRIDAY, MARCH 15, 2013

DANCING.

The last two hours of the Heels for Heaven charity gala are nothing but dancing.

That's why Adam's drinking tonight. At least, I guess that's why. Since dinner ended and the dancing started, I've stuck to one side of the ballroom, while Adam has been burning up the other.

It wasn't like this at galas past. Adam used to be a fabulous date. We would dance for hours, often commemorating our fun night by purchasing one of those cheesy dance floor snapshots: my head against his shoulder, Adam's round face lit up in a huge grin as he spun me.

And then we would go home. My house. Adam's condo. Maybe a hotel, if Adam was feeling dramatic and fun.

Wherever we landed, more often than not these last few years, trouble would start. I'd take care of Adam for hours as he lay on the bathroom floor, moaning and sweating. And in between bouts of being sick, he'd turn into someone mean; sometimes even cruel.

So, when he asked me to marry him a month ago, in a beautiful little ice cream shop in SOHO, I said yes—with a single stipulation: no more drinking.

Adam knows the extent of his issue—at least, I thought he did—because he didn't even bat an eye before agreeing.

I was on cloud nine that night. Adam, my sweetheart since our high school days at Hargrove Day School, told me he was moving back from New York. Opening his own one-man literary agency in San Francisco so I can continue to grow my interior design business. And the ring he gave me…

A three-carat diamond surrounded by itty bitty fire opals. It's so…*me*. Adam knows that. He knows everything about me.

So why is he on his sixth drink?

"You should just stop counting," Charlene says.

Charlene is my cousin. Our moms are sisters. We've traded secrets since toddlerhood, and we enjoy one of those comfortable relationships where we're able to pick back up after almost any length of time apart. Since I've chosen to keep Adam's drinking a secret from everyone else I know—I don't want people in our circle to judge him—I broke down tonight and told Charlene.

She's a watercolor artist, and she's jetting off to Sidney tomorrow afternoon for an extended showing, which is probably why I feel like I can confide in her. Unlike with my BFF, Lizzy DeVille—who's currently in Vegas—or my other BFF, Cross, who's in rehab after a major motorcycle accident, I won't have to talk about the situation with Charlene again for months.

"I'm not counting," I lie. "I was just…glancing over there."

Charlene scrunches her long, straight nose. "He must know you're pissed; he hasn't looked at you once in the last half-hour."

"Thanks, Char."

She slaps my back, bared by the low dip of my black, Swarovski-accented Atelier Versace gown. "Just stating the facts, cuz."

Maybe it *isn't* six drinks. Maybe it's only four or five. I tried very hard to not pay attention when he first started, so I could be off.

I glance at Charlene, who's waving her arm around in front of my face. "What did you just say?"

"I said, when's the wedding?" She tosses back some pinot grigio while wiggling her pale eyebrows.

"Oh, that. I'm not sure yet. I'll let you know when we decide."

"I will be flying home for it, wherever I happen to be," she says, leaning against the wall behind her.

I wrap my arm around her tall, lean form, hugging lightly. "Thanks, Char. That really means a lot to me."

She flashes me a thumbs-up, and seconds later, James Renfroe, from Charlene's class at Hargrove—two years ahead of me—struts over and jerks her into a funky waltz.

He winks at me and says, "You're next, Dalton," and then they're off, crisscrossing the shiny hardwood floor, weaving between more mild-mannered couples.

As I follow them with my eyes, I catch a glimpse of Adam. Regardless of how many drinks he's had so far, he's definitely tossing back another one just now.

I lean against the wall and grit my teeth. I don't get it. I picked him up from his townhouse tonight, and we had a nice time together on the ride here. True, we haven't seen each other for a week and a half—Adam isn't moving back to Cali for five weeks—but that seemed to make our time together better. Lots of snuggling and kissing. He seemed into it. I know I was.

Dinner was good, too: chicken breast saltimbocca, served with Anson Mills farro verde, organic bloomsdale spinach, La Quercia prosciutto, artichoke "chips" and a caper jus. We sat with the Davidsons and the Blancs, and it was easy-going and fun. I told a funny story about a San Francisco zoo fundraiser where a baby elephant knocked an aging socialite on her butt, and Adam seemed amused. He rested his hand on my knee under the table and gave me several just-for-Suri smiles.

And then the dancing started. I went to the ladies' room to adjust my tape-on bra cups, and when I got back, Adam was chatting up one of his college buddies and holding a glass of wine. I stuck around for a few minutes, saying "hi" to his friend, assuming Adam was only holding the drink for appearances. But then two more of Adam's buddies showed up, and he downed the first drink and a second in the space of five minutes. That was an hour and a half ago. Shortly thereafter, Charlene popped up, and I've been on this side of the room ever since.

The next hour passes in a miserable blur as I try to listen attentively to Charlene's Sidney plans. I dance a few times with various acquaintances and watch as Adam does the same, on the opposite side of the room. I watch him smile and laugh, animated and open, and I wonder what on earth his problem is. Does he plan to ignore me this way all night? People have surely noticed. Even worse, we said no drinking! Not because I'm a buzz-killing fiancé, but because Adam has a *problem*.

I'm on my second wine chute, wishing I could be like Adam and toss back five more in the next five minutes, when I see him gliding through the crowd. He stops to talk a few times, throwing his head back so his fluffy brown hair gleams in the dim globe lights. Smiling that handsome smile that makes him look so affable, so kind.

He strolls past a large, potted palm, smiling at me like nothing whatsoever is wrong, and when he's close enough so I can smell his cologne, he holds out his hand.

"A dance, my lady?"

I bite my lip, barely succeeding at holding back my tears. "Adam...I want to go."

"Home?" He bows lavishly at the waist, like an old-fashioned butler. "Then home it is."

He holds his arm out. I don't want to make a scene, so I

thread my hand through it, and together we walk to the club's valet room, where we stand in silence until one of the valets tells us the limousine is outside at the curb.

Adam leads me out the side door, down three brick steps to the curb line, and I can smell the alcohol on him.

My fingers burn holes in his worsted wool dinner jacket— one I've never seen. One he must have picked up in New York. And it occurs to me, as my body presses into his, that for the first time ever, I feel like I don't know him.

The club valet, Mark, opens the limousine's door for us. Adam waves his arm and I climb in, holding my gown so I don't snag or step on it. I settle on the far side of the limo, near the window, my clutch in my lap and my body language clearly telling him to stay the hell away. Adam hops in behind me, lithe and seemingly sober. But he's not fooling me. He gives Mark a little wink, and moves to close the door without handing out a tip.

"Hold on," I tell him. I reach across Adam, holding my arm out as a placeholder, and when Adam pauses, confused, I pull a twenty dollar bill out of my clutch.

"Thank you," I tell Tom, handing him the cash.

"Have a wonderful evening." He smiles and gently shuts the door.

I'm opening my mouth to say something to Adam—I'm not sure what, but something—when he leans back his seat, kicks his feet up on the partition, and gives me a silly grin. "Thanks, G."

I sink back into my seat and roll my eyes at my window. *Really? "G"?*

I feel the lurch of the car as Arnold takes off down the long, winding driveway, and I shut my eyes. I replay our conversation that night at Banana Beau's. Am I insane? Didn't I tell him no more drinking?

As I wrack my brain, Adam's clammy hand finds mine. I peek my eyes open, and of course, he can tell I'm irritated.

His thick eyebrows draw together, an exaggerated, drunken

expression of concern. "What's the matter, baby?" His pungent breath wafts over my face.

I'm not even sure where to start. I slide my hand out of his and drop my head into my palms. Maybe he forgot our agreement? Or did he simply start drinking because his old friends were there? Maybe he wanted to look 'normal'? If he can't withstand the pressure to drink around two men he rarely ever sees, he's not going to be able to honor this agreement of ours.

Well, obviously.

I think of the last time Adam and I went to a party—the Napiers' spring swing dance. We decided to stay at Adam's townhouse afterward. When I dared suggest Adam strip his vomit-covered clothes off and shower without—gasp—having sex first, he called me a bitch, and later that night, he called me a stupid whore.

"What's wrong?" he asks again.

I tremble with anger, but I keep my mouth pressed firmly closed. If he doesn't know, I'm not about to tell his drunken self.

His head falls on my shoulder, and he looks up at me through his eyelashes. "Don't be mad at me, Sur. We're gonna have a good night. You'll see."

I can't tell exactly how drunk he is, but it doesn't matter. He drank, and we said he wouldn't.

"I'm not so sure about that," I mumble, shaking him off me and scooting closer to the door.

I take a few deep breaths, gathering my patience. Preparing to discuss this whole drinking thing before Arnold gets much closer to my house, so if it turns into a fight, I can have him drop Adam off at Adam's townhouse.

I'm about to broach the subject when Adam leans over, opens up the mini fridge embedded in the partition wall in front of us, and pulls out a bottle of my favorite Aubert Pinot Noir.

He dangles it in front of my face. "Want to half it with me? Your favorite, baby."

"Of course not." I glare at him. "Do you have selective amnesia?"

He drops the wine into his lap and puts on his petulant, I-know-I-messed-up-and-now-I-can't-hide-from-it face as he makes another grab for my hand. I snatch it into my lap, setting my gaze on the partition in front of me. "Baby, I'm sorry. I won't do it again. I didn't have too much. I just needed…to loosen up, you know? You know how my social anxiety is."

Which is why I keep suggesting that he find himself a therapist.

I don't look at him. Not now, and not during the next fifteen minutes of our drive to Crestwood Place. I realize, belatedly, as we roll down my driveway, that Arnold brought Adam here, when I should have asked him to please take Adam home. I don't want to talk to Adam anymore tonight.

My eyes sting with tears as the limo stops, and I glance at him. He acts like such a child sometimes. How can I marry him if he's not willing to grow up? How can he really love me if he doesn't care enough about the drinking issue to just stop? Especially since he calls me ugly names when he gets drunk. My parents don't do that. Neither do my friends. Until Adam started drinking a lot, no one—*no one*—had ever called me any name.

I don't deserve that—right?

I think again about something my mother once told me: Most people never really change, and after marriage, bad habits tend to get worse.

Adam is leaning over his lap, with one elbow propped on his knee and his face in his hand, like he's upset. He hasn't touched the wine, but does that even matter? A tear spills down my cheek as I remember all the names he's called me during drunken moments—whore, bitch, cunt: things he would never call me when he's sober, but he's said them enough times when he's drunk that I'm convinced he's always thinking them.

How can I marry someone who thinks that I'm a cunt?

And isn't that a nasty little word?

I imagine my father's face. I would bet millions that he's never, *ever* called my mother a cunt. Even "bitch" seems hard to imagine coming from his lips. It should be unfathomable for Adam, too. What's wrong with him that it isn't? Or is it something wrong with me?

Am I a cunt?

I'm not, right?

Most people who know me think I'm nice. I have my moments, sure, but so does everyone.

I remember slamming the door of Adam's town house last time he drank. "If you name-call me again, I'm leaving you! I really am!"

Then he proposed and promised to quit.

I can no longer ignore my suspicion that he's been drinking in New York, too. Like, maybe almost every night. What happens when he moves to Napa? When we live together? I can't do this all the time!

As if he hears my thoughts, Adam raises his head and blinks at me.

"Adam," I say, "you need to go home. We'll talk tomorrow."

I expect contrition. Understanding. Instead, his eyes widen like I've slapped him. His shoulders square, and he reaches out to grab my elbow. "No way, baby. I want to get in the pool."

I frown. "You what?"

"Skinny dipping. It's your fantasy." He grins. "I'm feeling loose tonight. I think I can do it."

Adam's so uptight, he's never been willing to take a naked swim with me, not even when we've been the only ones at home.

"Lizzy's gone now," he says. "This is our night." He kisses the top of my hand. "Last night drinking. I fucking swear. I love you, baby. We can stop going to parties if we have to. I'll make the therapist appointment. Just let me swim with your fine self."

I struggle not to roll my eyes; then Adam kisses me gently on the lips. Despite the overwhelming scent of alcohol, I don't pull away when his arms wrap around me. He pulls me close to his chest—a signature Adam move that always makes me feel safe and sheltered—and for a long second, I can tell myself that he's my Adam. The guy I started dating in ninth grade. The one who could barely get a condom over himself when we lost it to each other in the fields behind Harvey Goldman's house.

I inhale his cologne and ignore the smell of the alcohol. I allow myself to ignore everything as he lifts me out of the limo and carries me around the back of my house. In the still of the night, I hear Arnold pull off, bound for the smaller, whitewashed house where he and the cook and my security guard have rooms.

The egg-shaped pool is crisscrossed by thousands of globe lights strung between the main house and the garden house. Tonight, the stars twinkle between them. It's beautiful.

"Adam," I say as he sets me gently on the pale tile. He looks down at me, and I wrap my arms around his neck and look at his familiar face. "It really hurt me that you did this after you promised you wouldn't."

I stare into his eyes, looking for some hint—any hint—that he gets it. That he understands why I'm upset.

He takes a step away from me and hangs his head, looking back up after a long moment staring at the Salvatore Ferragmo calfskin leather shoes I got him for his birthday. "I understand, Suri. I guess…I have a problem. Maybe I need to try AA or something."

Tension leaves me in a rush. I can feel my shoulders deflate like a popped balloon. "You'll actually consider that?"

"I guess I have to."

Yes!

I smile. I can't help it. "Adam, thank you. That makes me feel so much better."

"Anything for my girl." He grins and steps close enough to

kiss me quickly on the mouth, then starts stripping off his clothes.

My body temperature skyrockets. I can't help it. Adam is lean and cut. I'm not very tall—only five-foot-four—so at five-foot-ten, he's just my size. His blue eyes and mahogany hair look great with his naturally tanned skin. His grandmother is from Spain, and you can totally tell.

My mouth falls open when he tugs his boxers off, revealing a stiff erection.

"Ohh la la." I giggle and step over to him, and Adam does a deft job getting me out of my dress and slip. He kisses down my neck and over my bare shoulders. A brisk breeze blows, causing chills to pop up on my skin. He tweaks my hard, round nipple, and I gasp.

"Bad boy…"

He kneels, thumbing me through my panties before he pulls them down and tosses them over his shoulder. He takes my hand and leads me to the stairs at the shallow end of the heated pool. Steam drifts off the water, and I watch as it laps against Adam's knees, then thighs, then hips. He's submerged up to his chest when he turns and tugs me in behind him.

I sink down to my shoulders, glad my hair is swept up off my neck as I twirl around. It feels exquisite.

I look over at Adam. He's up to his pecs now, smiling a sweet smile, looking soft and attentive: the nice drunk he's never been.

"Come here baby." He holds his arms out, and my eyes fly to a bruise on his left shoulder, thinking for a second that he's finally gotten the tattoo I always fanaticize about.

Oh, well.

I step over to him, running my wet fingers through his hair and tugging his lips down on mine. As I do, I press my naked body against his and Adam groans a little.

"Baby… Oh yeah."

He starts kissing down my neck, just the way I like it. He kisses my collar bone and down my breast to my nipple, which he teases with his teeth. Through my haze of lust, I tell myself I'm not going to let his drinking ruin things for us. He'll go to AA. He did better tonight. He drank a lot in a brief time period and he's not calling me names.

One of his hands cups me in the water and he slides a finger in. I gasp, wriggling against him.

"You naughty, naughty boy."

I find him, too, stroking him as he moans.

He jerks out of my grasp, lifts me in his arms and presses my back against the side of the pool, lifting my legs so he can find my center. He spreads my lips, stroking twice before he takes himself in hand, and, holding onto the side of the pool, pushes inside of me.

It's supposed to feel good in the water, but I know after a couple of strokes it doesn't. I feel stretched too tight, and it stings.

He begins to thrust a little harder, kissing my mouth and stroking my neck with one hand as the other holds my hips.

"Oh, yeah…"

I bite my tongue, trying to get used to the sensation, but the pinching feeling just gets worse.

"Adam," I gasp. I push against his shoulder. "Stop, it hurts."

His eyes open, as he continues pumping. "Stop?"

"I'm really sorry, but it hurts."

He pulls out and lets go of me. I sink into the water while he spins around. "Damnit, Suri. This is bullshit!"

A shiver sweeps me as the wind blows. I wrap my arms around myself and hope he's just being a frustrated guy. This is *my* fantasy, after all. Something he's never felt comfortable doing. And I just shot him down.

Shoving my worries aside, I put on my sexy face and beckon him closer, curling my finger in a come-hither motion as the water laps around my shoulders. "Come here," I tell him, trying not to shiver as the breeze picks up. When he gets close enough, I'm going to grab his dick.

But he doesn't come. Instead, he turns around, running his hands roughly through his hair. "Jesus, you sure know how to kill a buzz."

"Come here, Adam." When he doesn't, I grab his bicep and turn him around. I grab his dick with one hand, stroking as my mouth finds his. He kisses me back roughly. Almost painfully, as if he's trying to bruise my lips. I try not to say "ow"—I don't want to put a damper on our sex life, especially when we only get to indulge several times a month—but he keeps it up, kissing so hard my teeth are almost cutting into my mouth, then moving down my neck and biting. Not sexy biting; real biting.

I can't help it. I push his shoulders. "Adam, stop!"

He shoves one wet hand into my hair, wrapping a strand around his fingers. "Come on, it's been a fucking week or maybe more."

He grabs my hips and pulls me closer to him, easing me toward the side of the pool again. Lifting me up, so the deck is digging into my back. Putting my legs atop his shoulders. He strokes my thigh and licks me twice, then pulls me abruptly back down into the water and enters me again.

Again, it stings. I'm not sure why. I close my eyes and try to loosen up, but eventually I have to squirm away. I push against him, looking up into his dazed eyes. "Adam, I'm really sorry. It just hurts."

He gives me a weird look, almost a sneer. It's not a look I see on him often, so I'm not sure what it means. He laughs a little. "Don't you want to be a good wifey?"

The comment is so ridiculously sexist and entitled, I can't believe it came from Adam's mouth. I'm so disgusted, I almost want to hit him. Instead, I splash him.

"You're being a jerk, just like you said you wouldn't be." I take a few steps back, already glancing at the stairs. There are no towels out here, but I don't care. All I want is to get inside, away from Adam and his issues.

Adam splashes me back, spraying water in my face. As I blink at him through my smeared mascara, I find he looks legitimately pissed off, as if I'm the one who's ruined our night.

"Fuck you," he mutters.

My jaw drops. I throw up my arms, shocked although I shouldn't be. "This is what you *always* do! You have a drinking problem, Adam!"

"Fuck you," he says again.

"Don't talk to me that way!"

He sneers. "I'll do what I want. You can't blame me. You're being a cock tease, Suri."

"And you can get out of my house!" I splash him one more time, because I'm furious, then wheel around and splash my way toward the stairs. Unable to just go, I turn around to find him standing there, still as stone. "You need to get a handle on yourself and grow up!"

I hustle onto the bottom stair, then up the second one, and am holding onto the railing, poised to take a third step, when Adam's hand closes around my left wrist. He doesn't yank me, but he grabs me with enough force that I lose my footing.

I try to take another step and lunge out of the pool, but of course he's got me by the arm, so I slip.

When I wake up, I'm lying on my back on the pool deck. My mouth is filled with blood, and one of my bottom teeth is embedded in my gum.

Adam is sorry, but I don't care.

That's the night I give the ring back.

Marchant

LAS VEGAS, NEVADA
FRIDAY, MARCH 15, 2013

I WISH RACHELLE would quit blowing up my phone. I should be grateful that she's calling me rather than tromping over from the main house and banging on my front door—but I'm not. Not at all.

I toss the phone onto the mattress and drop my head down on my pillow. Close my eyes. Try to get back to the peaceful nothingness I was drifting through.

Sometime later, I sit up, because I can't.

Of course I can't.

Seven years, and it never gets easier.

Sorrow flows through me like poison. Sorrow and sickness. Sorrow and sickness and disgust and horror—and regret. So, so much regret.

Even with my eyes open, staring at the framed ace of spades on my bedroom wall, I see her. What she might look like now. The color of her hair…her eyes.

I look down at my bare chest, at the script along the lower left side of my ribcage, crawling vertically up me, just above my hip to just below my heart.

March 15, 2007.

It's March 15 today, and it can't be over soon enough.

I lean over, grab my phone, and shoot Rachelle a text: *Got the flu; pretend you're me. You have carte blanche, woman. Use it.*

Hoping the text seems "normal," I sag back against my army of maroon pillows. Let my eyes drift shut. Enjoy the way that gravity drags down on me, keeping me from moving. I don't want to move.

Except the fucking phone is ringing again, and it's not the Icona Pop ringtone Rachelle attached to her name. I grab the thing, flopping onto my back and holding it up over my face. Libby.

I press the fuck you button. Drop my arm on my chest. The phone vibrates when she leaves a message. Second one today.

I wonder dully about the likelihood that she'll hunt me down. Then, from the depths of my cloudy memory comes a convenient bit of information: Libby is leaving for France on Friday, to visit her daughter.

Friday is today.

How long will she be gone?

Two weeks? Four?

I sit up again and rub my blood-shot eyes. I can't remember.

That should make me concerned. I should hear alarm bells peeling from somewhere through the fog. But I don't. Because I just can't seem to make myself care. About anything. And least of all, me.

I slide my tired ass off the bed and walk slowly to my bathroom, where I open the medicine cabinet and remove several unlabeled bottles of prescription pills: my dirty little secret. I pour one bottle into the palm of my hand and stare at all the little round, white tablets. I wonder how many swallows it would take to choke all of them down.

Since I've forbidden drop-bys to my garden house behind the three main Love Inc. buildings, it'd probably be a while before I was found. I'm the one in charge here. I'm the boss. No one would defy me. Not because I'm an ass (although I can be). It's because they're all so goddamn well-paid. I've learned the best way to ensure loyalty is with lots of the green stuff; everybody at Love Inc. ranch is very loyal.

I'm still staring at my hand when the doorbell rings.

I roll my eyes and toss the pills into the toilet.

It rings again.

Go away, Libby. I'm not gonna answer you today.

I sigh and find my phone. Type out a text. *Got the flu. Hook up next week? Skype?*

Even finding the question mark key on my phone is so fucking wearying.

I hit 'send', then grab the other two bottles and empty them into the toilet.

This shit is over. It's not working anymore. I need something else.

A good lay, maybe, or a game of blackjack. A fucking drink. Maybe something a little bit stronger just to pick me up.

And that's how I end up at Tao, in the back room with the high rollers, gambling away two million dollars I don't exactly have.

That's also how I end up snorting a couple lines of coke and fucking twins named Elise and Elsbeth.

I feel on top of the world by the time I'm zipping up my pants. When that little fucking twerp Rex Hawkins finds me outside the men's room and asks for what I owe him, I don't give a shit. I laugh and tell him, "Later. I've gotta move the funds from the money market."

The money is there; it's just hard to get to. I give him one of my business cards, the little red ones with the sexy Love Inc. logo.

"You need it sooner, come to my place." It's a challenge, and he knows it.

I barely even feel it when one of his thugs smashes his fist into my face.

I'm up again. I'm back in business. The clock just struck midnight.

March 16.

CHAPTER TWO

Suri

NAPA, CALIFORNIA
FRIDAY, APRIL 19, 2013

THE FIRST THING I notice is how gross my mouth feels. I swish my tongue over my teeth: unbrushed. Ugh.

I lift my head and find myself at the work desk in my bedroom. My stiff neck protests as I turn to search for the wall clock. Based on how tired I feel, and by the dim light filtering through the long, pale green curtains, I'm guessing it's still early. Which is why, when I see the actual time, I shriek.

"Aaaaaaaaaaaaaaah!"

I'm up and running to my bathroom, because it's nine fifteen. I have an appointment in the vineyard in less than an hour. Still, there's time to shower. Something quick, and I'll let my curly, brown hair air-dry on the drive over to the Bernards' country home. I lean over to turn the shower faucet, my hair falls over my shoulder, and out of the corner of my eye, I notice a web of pink that makes my blood run cold.

I whirl around, fully facing the wide, long mirror and seriously almost cry. That pink stuff is bubble gum. I fell asleep chewing bubble gum, and now it's in my hair!

"AAAAAAAAAAAAAAAAAH!"

I pick and pull at the mess, but it's overtaken the entire left side of my head. I glance around the bathroom, searching for a clock that isn't here. Of course I don't have time for an emergency trip to Julian, my stylist. But I can't go to the clients' house with gum in my hair. It's a consult. They won't hire me if I look like a crazy bag lady.

"Damn, damn, damn!" I tug open a drawer, grab my small, stainless steel scissors, and get to chopping. Fifteen minutes later, I'm dressed in a red Armani pants suit with a slouchy fedora. Underneath it, my now-straight hair hangs just a little bit below my chin.

My shoulders feel too light. My face looks blunt and sharp and not like me.

I grab my makeup bag and dash out the front door, down the porch, toward my lilac Land Rover, still dotted with dew under an overcast sky.

I know for sure I'm having "one of those days" when a bird smacks into my windshield before I even get out of my driveway. It's cute and small and brown, and based on the tailspin it takes in the wake of the Land Rover, I'm guessing I just punched its ticket to bird heaven.

Lovely.

As I jet from Crestwood Place, a columned, brick home on one-hundred acres just outside downtown Napa, to the valley, I try driving with my knees, something my father absolutely loathes and something I've never been great at. I manage to run off the road once, smear my eyeliner (top and bottom) on my right eye, and put on the wrong color eye shadow, so I appear to be going for an emo look.

Lovely.

When I'm finished with my makeup, I flip the mirror up, press the pedal to the floor, and turn up some Florence and the Machine, holding onto the wheel as I fly down hills, around curves, past acres and acres of grapes. I make it to the Bernards' house only two minutes after our set appointment time of ten o'clock.

The crumminess of the day is once again confirmed when I climb out, briefcase on my shoulder, smile polished and ready, to find Dr. and Mr. Bernard standing several feet apart in their freshly sodded lawn, screaming obscenities at each other.

Behind them, their sprawling Tuscan-style home stands empty, waiting for my finishing touch, but as their heads whip to me in unison, I know it's not going to happen.

"Miss Dalton." Mr. Bernard strides forward, trying to greet me, and his wife throws a wine glass at his shoulder. It shatters, falling in glittering pieces to the lawn as my mouth drops open. He turns around. "Honey, now is not the time or—"

"Yes it is the time!" Her shoulders are heaving, her long blonde hair bouncing down her back. She's wearing scrubs, no makeup, and she looks like she wants to murder her husband. "You lying, cheating, small-dicked bastard—"

"Miss Dalton," Mr. Bernard starts. "Perhaps another—"

"No." The woman turns to me. "No other time. This is my money, my vacation house, and he won't get a thing after I divorce his cheating ass!" Panting, she quickly gathers herself and adds, "Sorry, Suri. We'll have to try this another time. Give your mother my regards."

I stand there only a second longer before Mr. Bernard turns to go inside. His wife intercepts him, shoving him toward the garage. "Don't you even think if stepping foot into *my* home you fucking asshole."

Just great. I lost this job. I don't have another booking until mid-May. This leaves me with enough to pay the essentials, but not as much as I need if I'm going to save for a trip to Paris in the winter.

And—damnitty damn!—I cut my own hair for these people. Because I didn't think I had time to get to Julian's.

My shoulders slump. I climb into my car. Turn down the

Florence. Turn up some Bon Iver. But listening to Bon Iver while driving out of the valley reminds me of my good friend Cross Carlson. Cross, who last November had a motorcycle accident on one of these very vineyard roads. Cross, who a mere week ago was the recipient of my... My what? My desperate advance? My half-naked body and enthusiastic lips? My dashed dreams? My fledgling hopes? I roll my eyes at myself and turn down the music. I'm sick and tired of replaying the sad scenario with Cross. Putting the moves on him was a stupid thing to do—one I probably wouldn't have done had I not still been in a state of shock and alarm over the way things ended with Adam.

Adam.

Ugh.

I'm tired of thinking about Adam, too, and I'm tired of slow, sad songs.

I roll the windows down, find some Sara Bareilles, and am headed toward Julian's studio when my mother calls. I hit ignore. She calls again. And calls, and calls, and calls.

I sigh and answer. "Do you need me, Mom?"

"I do, as a matter of fact. Where are you, darling?"

"Leaving the Bernards' house."

"Oh that's right. How did it go?"

More than thirty years of being married to an uber secretive tech tycoon has made my mother very discreet—or maybe she always was. I give her a quick rundown of the situation at the Bernards' house, figuring she'll hear it soon enough from Dr. Bernard, anyway, since the two are good friends. I'm almost to Julian's, and am feeling a little less pessimistic about the world, when Mom asks, "So...are you going to New York?"

I nearly choke.

"You haven't asked to use the jet this weekend."

"That's true," I hedge. "I thought I might just...go commercial this time. You know, since I've used the jet so much this last year."

I can almost see her jaw drop over the phone line. "Book and *board*? Well, what time are you leaving, darling? You know, there may not be anything left in first class." Her voice lilts up on "first class," as if this is a catastrophic possibility.

"I know, Mom. But I can handle business class." I've flown that way a time or two, and I've yet to get pick-pocketed, infected with scabies, or kidnapped for ransom. "I *am* a business owner," I remind her.

"I know." It's half sigh; again, like this is a shame. "I assume you're on your way there now?"

"Um, in just a little while." *Not.* I'm an outright liar now. I blink at the tidy buildings around me, feeling like a goldfish on a rug.

"Well aren't you going to miss the big event?"

I exhale slowly, tightening my grip on the steering wheel. "Mom, what event?" I know I'm busted before the words leave my mouth, but what am I to do? I'm not keeping up with Adam anymore. It's unhealthy.

"I knew it," my mother cries. "Something is going on with you and Adam!"

"Is it?"

"He has a book signing at the Time Square Bookseller in three hours, Suri."

Despite myself, I feel my stomach flip. "What do you mean, a book signing?"

"For the décor book, darling. The one you and he thought up. For the series?"

Sweat prickles under my hairline. "What series?"

"The series of home books on...crafting and art and, *you* know. I noticed the write-up in the *Times* didn't mention your name. I thought it was a joint project. What's going on, darling?"

What's going on is Adam stole my idea. *My* idea. Sure, we talked about my idea together—a series of simple, colorful coffee table books on home décor and cooking. I'd originally thought of them as fun gifts for my clients, but Adam had urged me to dream bigger. "This could be a hit. Like HGTV," he'd said. "Everyone is interested in this stuff. It's really hot right now."

We outlined the chapters for the home décor book on a weekend trip to La Jolla. Or rather, I did. I left the notes in his Audi, and when we started to argue over the outlines for the second, third, and fourth books, Adam suggested we drop the project.

I bite down on my lower lip. That was almost a year and a half ago! Adam poached my idea before we even got engaged!

"Suri, darling—"

"We broke up, mother. Okay? A few weeks ago, right before you had your bunion surgery, Adam and I decided to break things off. I told Rachel and Edith, and I asked them not to tell you because I was waiting for the right time." I'd known it would take the news a while to reach my mother, who'd been confined to bed for several weeks after her surgery.

She sniffs. "It's clear the right time never came. How long were you going to wait, darling?"

"Of course it didn't come. Who wants to talk about things like this?" My hands, around the steering wheel, tighten as I turn right at a red light.

"Suri, I'm your *mother*. Does your father know?" I can tell by her voice that she'd be more annoyed if he did, so I'm relieved that I can tell her, "No. I haven't told him yet."

"I can't believe this. Suri, it's just terrible! What *happened*, darling?"

I pull into the parking lot of a retro-looking building that houses, among other things, Julian's. I lean down and put my forehead against the steering wheel and sigh, like I'm five years old and being asked to eat my green beans. "Mom, if you want the full story, can you just ask Rachel? I don't feel like going into it right now."

"You can't tell me *anything*?"

I sigh again and close my eyes. "I can tell you it just wasn't right, for either one of us. We'd been together so long we didn't know it, but I don't think I was what he really wanted, and I don't think he's what I want."

This isn't the real reason things ended, of course—it ended with me hurling my ring at Adam's head, where it bounced off and landed in the pool—but I'm surprised to find it definitely *feels* true. Adam wants a dandelion, someone who bends with him and doesn't ask questions. I want...well, I want someone who's not an ass. Someone who doesn't have a drinking problem. Someone who's spontaneous and fun. Someone who actually wants to live in the same state as me. (Adam felt coerced, I think, into moving back to California). Someone who likes to go down on me. (Adam never did—not really). Someone who'll eat a cheeseburger and go flying in a hot air balloon with me. (Adam only ate steak, and he hated heights).

My mother clucks. "I'm truly sorry to hear that, Suri. I'm sure it's been difficult for you. I'll try not to feel insulted that you didn't tell me sooner."

"Please do try. It's me, not you. I mean it."

"Oh, I understand." She says this as if maybe she actually doesn't. "That does explain why you haven't been asking to use the jet. You're not flying business class at all, are you?"

"Not this weekend, but that doesn't mean I don't or won't."

"Of course not. In the event of an emergency."

"Right." I roll my eyes. After reassuring my mom I'll call her if I need her, I'm off the phone and staring at the front of Julian's building. I should just get out and go inside and show him the mess I've made of myself.

Instead, I hold out my left hand, where today I'm wearing one of my grandmother's emerald rings, and I flip down my visor's mirror to take a look at the tiny plastic tooth sitting where my lower left incisor used to be. It got knocked out the night I fell, and after Adam finally called a taxi home, I had to drive myself to Edith's boyfriend's house so he could give me a stitch inside my lip. He's a resident at the local hospital, and thank god he keeps a first aid kit at his house. The official line to Edith was that I got so mad at Adam, I ran into a doorframe. I think she believed me. No one would ever dream that Adam could be mean to me. Not affable, gentlemanly Adam.

Just the memory of that night leaves me feeling exhausted and discouraged, so I guess I walk into Julian's looking down and out. His assistant, Sally, gets me a glass of lemonade and two shortbread cookies, and sets about getting someone to give me a back rub while I wait for Julian to finish the client he's working on.

When he finally sees me, Julian slaps both hands to his cheeks and starts to laugh. Which makes me laugh a little. "That bad, huh?"

"What happened?"

"Bubble gum," I tell him solemnly.

I spend the next hour getting cut and dyed and styled. As usual, I don't glance in the mirror until he's finished. When I do, I gasp.

"Julian, you made me *blonde*!"

"Not blonde. I brought out your eyes with highlights."

I cackle insanely, because while maybe he did, he also made me look even more un-me than I looked before.

"I look like…"

"A model? Yes you do." His brown eyes shine.

"A model," I say slowly. And it's kind of true. The hair's that good.

I fling my arms around Julian's neck and he pats my head. "I heard about your nasty break-up, doll."

Wow. "You did? From who?" I haven't told anyone hardly, and I didn't think Adam had either.

"Brina Lulle came in the other day."

My stomach sinks at the mention of the petite dancer from our high school class. "She's going for him, isn't she?"

Julian shrugs. "You didn't hear it from me."

"Promise," I say, holding up my hand.

I drive home feeling... I don't know. Betrayed? *I* broke up with *him*, and even though I think it's what we both needed, Adam certainly didn't agree when we spoke last, three days after that night at the pool. He's probably embarrassed. Hurt. He's probably saying he broke it off with me.

I didn't expect him to spend a year in a monastery or anything, so it shouldn't bug me—the idea of him and Brina; and my post-break-up track record is blighted by my embarrassing attempt to seduce a friend, after all.

But I'm lying if I say it doesn't.

I shift my attention to the darkening clouds above the county road that leads from town to my house. A few seconds later, a misty rain begins to fall.

I try to feel normal. To feel okay. But I can't shake the pessimism, the nauseating unease that's been following me like these storm clouds for the last few weeks.

What bothers me, I think, as I ride toward my empty house, is how far I am from where I thought I'd be right now. Not with the business. Northern California Interiors is doing better than I could have hoped, and believe me, I'm grateful for that. I'm much different than Mom, who seems satisfied doing the cliché wife thing: charity ball this, gala for the children that. Her work actually is important, but I find so many of those things boring.

I'm glad I'm getting to do what I enjoy, and I'm glad I had a good enough year last year that I was able to buy Crestwood Place from my parents. I don't like freeloading, and I wanted to make the home mine officially. I was able to help my best friend Lizzy by offering her a room here, rent free, before she met Hunter West—the heir to the West Bourbon fortune, a savvy investor, and, as of several weeks ago, Lizzy's fiancé. That makes me happy, too. So life's not all bad.

The bad part is losing the sense of pride I had whenever I would think of what a great pair Adam and I were. We'd been together since ninth grade, and everything about Adam was familiar and comfortable—at least until it wasn't. I've wasted years feeling content and settled with Adam, and now I have nothing to show for it. I don't like being single, not because it's un-fun, but because it makes me feel off-balance. Like a bike with one tire flat. And yet, when I think of dating anyone, it's the last thing I want to do.

I'm about to turn into my driveway when I remember it's midday on a Friday, meaning the gym where Lizzy and I learned Tai Chi has an open sparring hour.

I am *so* going to that.

I do, and it feels good, and afterward I'm driving home when Lizzy calls. She's in Vegas, where she's been shacked up with her fiancé, Hunter, for the last few weeks. She claims to be happy at the casino where Hunter has a penthouse, but today I can tell something's bothering her.

"Suri...hi. What's up?"

"Driving home from Tai Chi."

"Oh, the happy hour thing?"

"Yep. Felt good, too." I don't tell her it felt good because I imagined I was sparring Adam. I haven't told anyone what happened that night at the pool. No one except my cousin even knows he had—*has*—a drinking issue. It's not that I never plan to tell...it's just I can't bring myself to talk about it yet.

"I'm jealous," Lizzy says, and I remember we're talking about the gym.

I wipe a trail of sweat from my temple and stick my tongue out at the phone. "Maybe you should come see your BFF, then."

"Maybe you should come see me. Like, say, tonight?" I know Lizzy, and despite the on-its-face simplicity of her suggestion, I can tell something's up.

"Tonight? Have you been deserted by your man?"

"Yeah, he's got that charity Hearts tournament I mentioned the other day." Hunter West is a professional poker player. I wonder how he does at Hearts.

"So you're looking for a girls' night?"

"Something like that." I can practically see her chewing her lip, the way she does when she's nervous.

I'm about to press her for details, but she says, "What do you think? Could you come short-notice? We could try the slots. I could even take you to Love Inc. to meet the girls."

I make a face, and I guess she's as good at imagining my face as I am hers, because Lizzy says, "Just kidding. Kind of."

Love Inc. is the high-end brothel where she auctioned her virginity. The place is owned by this guy named Marchant Radcliffe, who happens to be Hunter's fratty best bro from Tulane.

I've glimpsed the guy at a party or two, and he always seems so...pimpish. Don't get me wrong: He's got amazing clothes, and from what little I've seen of him, he's not hard on the eyes—wild, brown-blond-red hair he wears kind of spiky, and a sexy beard—but he's got a certain swagger I just can't tolerate. Like he has sex with a different woman every night and he's just so...proud of himself. Like he owns two huge brothels, filled with women willing to satisfy any man's sex fantasies.

Oh wait—he *does* have two huge brothels filled with women willing to satisfy any man's sex fantasies!

I wrinkle my nose. "No thanks on that part." I'm sure Lizzy's new escort friends are nice and all, but...they're escorts. "But I'd love to come see you at the casino. I finally let the cat out of the bag about Adam to my mom today, so I'm sure the jet will be ready at a moment's notice. She'll probably think I need some girl time."

"Oh my God, you finally told Gretchen..."

And so begins an hour-long conversation, during which I tell Lizzy all about my day and she tells me absolutely nothing about hers. In fact, the longer I talk to her, the more convinced I am that something's going on. I consider asking her outright, but while we're on the phone I send my mom an e-mail, which she answers immediately from her iPhone, letting me know the jet can be ready in an hour. She hopes I have a wonderful weekend, where I focus on just me! Smilie face!

Soon I'll be in Vegas, and I'll find out what Lizzy is hiding.

MY MOOD PLUMMETS as I pack. My iPhone's calendar alerts me at exactly four o'clock that it's time to take an ovulation test. If I were going to ovulate this month, my doctor thinks today would be the day. Actually, I can't believe I haven't taken the test already. It's a testament to how scattered I am lately. For the last six months, since I've been working with an expert OB-GYN in Beverly Hills, I haven't ever forgotten to take the test on O-Day. Of course, there hasn't ever *been* an O-Day, so maybe I forgot today because I've finally given up.

My reproductive system is a lemon. I've got two ovaries, but they don't release eggs monthly. I got my period for the first time when I was sixteen, and I had it until I turned nineteen, when it disappeared, never to return.

I drop a strapless bra and a blouse into my suitcase and trudge into the bathroom, where a quick test confirms what I already knew: I'm not ovulating today.

Woohoo.

Most months, I spend hours obsessing over what this means for me; what this meant for Adam and me. Today, I just don't have the energy.

I toss the test in the garbage can, push my purse onto my shoulder, hoist my hang-up bag over my other shoulder, and drag my rolling suitcase to the elevator.

Arnold gives me a ride to my family's airport, not much

more than two hangars in a giant field between Napa and the valley. On the way, I make like Adam and pop the cork on a bottle of Pinot Noir. Stupid Clomid. Stupid all the other drugs I've tried. Stupid Dr. Haynes. Stupid ovaries.

I guess it's a good thing I'm single now. I'm never going to give any man children.

I shut my eyes and take a few deep swigs straight out of the bottle. And when we arrive at the airport, I stuff the bottle into my purse—probably just like Adam, too, if he carried a purse.

I focus on the feeling of my legs moving as they carry me from the limousine to the blue and grey Boeing Dad bought when I was in high school. I pay attention to my arms as they clutch my luggage. I clench my stomach underneath my shirt. I think about my ovaries below my stomach.

What's wrong with me? So far, nobody knows. Maybe I don't care, I think as I hike up the plane's fold-out stairs. Maybe I'll be an old maid with a hundred cats. Or dogs, because cats are just difficult.

Even the thought of a hundred darling dogs depresses me, and as soon as I see our family's long-term flight attendant, Esmerelda, I realize that, just like at Julian's earlier, I must be wearing my mood all over my face. She throws her arms around me and leads me to the most comfy, recliner-style seat on the jet, and starts a movie on the flatscreen right in front of me: *Finding Nemo*.

"You need something fun today," she declares.

I just nod, because really, what else can I say? Nemo is perfect. He's got the little fin; I've got the broken ovaries.

"Would you like a drink?"

I must look like shit. I laugh and pull out the bottle of Pinot Noir from my Belkin bag.

She laughs, too. "Oh, so it's a bad, bad day."

I nod again, feeling too tired to think of anything to say, and she takes the bottle and brings me a glass filled with the crimson liquid.

For the next two hours, Esmerelda refills my glass…a lot of times. Every time I finish, she refills it. I toss them back just like Adam, and watch the little orange fish swim around the screen with a strange, dull feeling—like I'm living inside an empty aquarium.

When we touch down at the private airport behind the Wynn Casino, in downtown Vegas, Esmerelda laughs at me, and ruffles my newly styled, short hair. "I never seen you drunk, Suri Dalton."

I blink blearily at her. "I don't ever get drunk."

"I didn't think you did." She squeezes my arm. "Would you like me or Lonnie—" that's the pilot— "to walk with you?"

I shake my head, feeling the plane tilt around me. "Um, no. I'm fine."

"If you're sure," she says.

I catch a glimpse of lights outside the window, then point weakly to the bags, and Esmerelda nods. "We'll get them to Mr. West's room. Don't worry."

"Thank you."

As I float toward the plane's door, she says, "Go have some fun!"

I tell her I will, and hold on tightly to the railing as I make my way down the stairs in my sexiest jeans, red Lanvin ballet flats, and a flowy white Marc Jacobs blouse I got last time I went shopping on Rodeo Drive.

I wander toward the glossy-looking high-rises with only my purse on my shoulder, and it's then I realize I have no idea where I'm going. I've only been to Hunter's penthouse once, and in my drunken state, I can't seem to understand how the trees and grass around me will lead me back there.

I look around. I'm past the airport now and on a…golf course? I giggle. This is not good. I suck at golf. I can't see Hunter West in a golf shirt. Pretentious Casual—that's what I'll call his style. Lizzy sold her clubs when her dad left so she can't play, either. Golf sucks! I twirl around. There are palm trees strung with lights. So many lights! They make me dizzy!

I ended up sitting on one of the greens, but a rescuer arrives! A golf cart is here. There's a man in a suit. He's saying, "Can I help you?"

I blink up at him and grin. "My prince charming!"

We strike a deal, and he says he will take me out of the palm tree forest, to the Wynn.

"And you work here?" I ask him for the first—or second?—time.

"Yes, miss. I'm a ball boy."

I giggle. Balls.

"*Golf* balls."

He chuckles. "*Golf* balls."

He presses the pedal, and I get dropped into the rabbit hole. Lots of lights and pools that glow and other lights, and umbrellas and stuff hanging over gardens, and I see some dancers wearing feathers on their butts and I think I saw a waterfall peeking through the brush.

There's this lighted path, and we drive down it, and then we're standing in front of this Zen-ish garden place, and there's a bunch of tropical trees and a stone path and tables with candles where people are eating stuff that smells good, kind of like tuna, and my guide is biding me au revoir. I'm out of the cart, standing along a tree-lined path. My legs feel shaky.

"Wait—but what do I do now?" I turn around. My guide is gone. I'm by myself.

Oh, God.

I'm not sure how I make it to the penthouses. I'm on the 46th floor, and the view from the back of the glass elevator makes me dizzy. I step onto the shiny chocolate marble, under big, round, gold chandelier things, and I have a hazy memory of tipping someone pretty generously and mentioning Hunter's name.

But uh-oh. There's a problem. This hallway, where the elevator dropped me off, only has one door, and it's guarded by a solid gold lion. I blink my bleary eyes and try to see it in a different light, but I know décor, and this does not say 'Hunter' or 'Lizzy' to me. Not at all.

I sink down against the wall, stick my cold hands into my bag, and give my fine motor skills a challenge by searching for my makeup. I giggle as I pop open a compact and refresh my lipstick—see, I don't look drunk!—and stumble as I get back to my feet. I drop the makeup back into my purse and fish my iPhone out. I dial Lizzy's number, still smiling stupidly, but when it goes to voice mail, my stomach starts to feel sick.

I'm lost.

I'm lost in a big casino. Not just a casino. A casino wonderland, with an Alexander McQueen boutique and waterfalls and flashy lights and steam and marble and glittery diamond lamps.

"Where is Lizzy?" I whisper to myself.

I'm back at the big, brass elevator, repeatedly banging the 'down' arrow. The doors open a couple seconds later, and I ride to the main floor, where I'm dizzied again by the sights, sounds, and smells of the casino.

The décor is glossy and rich, with bold, bright colors, varied textures and fabrics, gazillion-foot ceilings, and expansive, art-lined corridors. If I'm not mistaken, Roger Thomas did the last remodel, and I think it's...amazing. I'm scrutinizing his extravagant potted plant choices when it dawns on me that I should try to call Lizzy again.

I do, and it's the same as last time: no answer after several rings, then voicemail.

I pick a comfortable looking, bumblebee yellow couch and sink down onto it. "Lizzy," I hiss into the phone, "I'm down in the casino, and I need you. Where are you?"

I hang up, feeling tears burn in my eyes, and decide I'm not going to be some drunk girl crying in a casino lobby. Maybe I can walk off my buzz and figure out how to get to Hunter's penthouse.

Figure it out?

I should just go ask!

Du-huhhh.

I cut through a few private casino rooms filled with people doing special things—oops—and finally make it to an information desk, where I ask a stern-looking middle-aged guy about Hunter West's penthouse.

He frowns at me. "Ma'am, we don't give out our residents' information without prior resident authorization."

"But...can't you just call him?"

"I suppose I can try."

No dice.

When he hangs up the phone, I'm feeling desperate. "You're sure?"

He nods.

I narrow my eyes at the man, then press my lips together and lean forward a little. Lower my voice, in case bad people are around. "Sir...I don't mean to be a diva, but...I'm not a bad person. I'm not a *criminal*. That's what I mean." I'm floundering. I stand straighter, throw my shoulders back. Pretend I'm not drunk. "My father is Trent Dalton. You know, the computer guy?" I raise my eyebrows.

"I know who Trent Dalton is, ma'am. Everyone does."

I smile a little. "Okay, so, then, it's okay to let me into Hunter West's room. *Up to* his room, I mean. Up to. Not *into*."

"I'm sorry ma'am. Not without prior resident authorization."

I nod a few times before turning away.

I call Lizzy two more times without success.

"This is a bad day," I murmur to myself. "Bad night. This is a bad month."

A few minutes later, I'm dawdling near a vast room decorated like the pages of a Japanese manga and filled with slot machines, when a bulky man in a staff suit grabs my elbow.

"Ma'am, may I help you?"

I shake my head, removing my elbow from his presumptuous grasp. "No, I don't need anything."

He frowns at me, looking suspicious, and I sigh. "I'm looking for some friends, but I'll find them eventually. Maybe."

His eyebrows—dark, I notice—scrunch like fuzzy caterpillars. "Ma'am, are you intoxicated?"

I blink, surprised by the question. "Is that abnormal? This is a casino!" I hate to be terse, but I don't appreciate his manner.

His hand grasps my elbow again. "Please come with me, Miss. We can get this sorted out at the security station."

"Is this a joke?" I tug against his grasp, trying to wrap my addled mind around what he's telling me. "Did I get paged or something?"

His fingers, locked around my wrist now, are almost crushing. "Come with me now, Miss. We'll get this sorted out when we get there."

I bite my lip, looking him over as he walks half a step ahead of me. My eyes dart all around the hall, crammed with thrill-seekers of every nationality, gender, and age. I can't find anyone dressed in a uniform like this man's, and I'm too buzzed to remember what the other employees were wearing.

All my mother's warnings play in my head like a recording stuck on a loop. All the things she's told me about being kidnapped. Dad's wealth is notable. *And I told them who I am!*

With my heart pounding, I jerk my hand away. "I'll need to see some ID, sir."

With my heart pounding, I jerk my hand away. "I'll need to see some ID, sir." I back away from him, already glancing around for somewhere to run if he acts shady.

Time seems to hang in place, the bright, loud scene around me freezing as my heart gallops.

The man rushes forward to grab me, looking meaner—more sinister—than he did before, and that's all it takes. I turn and run.

CHAPTER THREE

Marchant

WHEN JENKINS STOPS the Bentley at the doorway of the Wynn, I'm still working on my blunt.

"Hey dude, we're here," Jenk calls over his shoulder. He's got some new tracks thumping, and with his tortoiseshell glasses and his toothpaste commercial smile, he looks a little ridiculous: my 20-year-old chauffeur. The deal is, I pay for his college and he drives me around to shit like this. Call me crazy, but I need it to be someone younger than me. I feel like hell every time I see an old guy driving someone. Shouldn't he be fly fishing or watching *Andy Griffith* or some shit?

I didn't stab the cherry out when I pressed the blunt into the ash tray, so I take another quick hit and nod as smoke pours out my nostrils. "Yeah, I noticed." The flickering blue glow of the pools in front of the casino makes this difficult to miss.

I straighten my jacket and fuck with my tie and run my fingers through my newly trimmed beard. I don't want to get out, but...I kind of have to.

I tuck the .38 in my pants pocket as I reach for the door handle, and Jenk reaches back and slaps my shoulder. "You want me to wait around, right?"

I blink at him, replay his words, then shake my head. "Nah.

Go home and study, man. You've got…finals?"

He laughs. "Two weeks ago."

"What?" I rub my dry eyes, trying to make sense of this.

"Two weeks ago. Finals already happened, dude. I'm on a break right now, so I can wait as long as you need."

I shake my head again. "Park her at the Sahara location and go home. I'll call a cab or something."

"You sure?"

Goddamn, this kid is persistent. I cut my eyes at him, trying not to let my foul mood show. "Yeah, man. I got it."

That's a lie. But I still owe a guy some money, and I don't need to involve the kid in whatever might happen. What is it they say? Bad impression. No—it's bad *example*. Kids are vulnerable, and I'm an example, right?

It's Friday night—still early, but the Wynn is hopping. The weed keeps me mellow, so the crowd doesn't bother me much. I hurry through the massive, marble-columned hallway, trying to keep my head down as I walk toward the private room that's reserved for the Hearts for Heroes fundraiser Hunter roped me into. It's for the cardiac unit at the local children's hospital, and there's some elaborate system they're using to raise the money. Something with teams. We're calling ours the Love Inc. team, even though Hunter set everything up, and we've got a couple of extra people.

I feel like an asshole with this gun in my pocket, and I'll look like one if security sees it, but I can't take the risk of getting jumped by Hawkins. Rex Hawkins, the guy who's been threatening to shoot me in the back.

Fuck him. I said I would pay. I just need a little longer to get the money moved. Fuck Hawkins for starting that fight last week at Tao. Fuck Tao, too. I got a month-long ban and a ride to the South MLK police station, and Hawkins got nothing.

I try to shove my anger down as I turn sideways to get past a group of Asian men in pastel business suits. I need to keep my mind on tonight, not get lost in that other shit. But I can't help it; I wish I was at Tao playing blackjack. I wish I could find Rex Hawkins and kick his fucking ass.

I press my hand against my pocket and remind myself that guns are terrible things. I'm not a gun guy, right? I'm all about the party.

I should throw the gun out.

Where? A trash receptacle? No *way*. The cameras pick that shit up. I rub my slacks again, but my mind is fucking hazy. I don't know what to do with the damn thing.

The room we're in is big, with high ceilings, floor-to-ceiling windows, marble floors, and lots of black, fringed chandeliers that look, to me, like video-game monsters. Tonight the lights inside of them are glowing red. I guess in honor of the whole Hearts thing.

Kids with heart defects. Now that shit is sad. Really god-damned sad. When I think about the kids, I need a fucking drink.

This dude comes up, and I swear I've got some magic fuck-ing powers, because he's got a tray loaded with alcohol. I grab what looks like Long Island iced tea and down it before he can make it to the next person.

"Let me grab another one, dude." I shove a hundred into his palm and grab two more drinks.

"One for my friend," I mutter as I step away.

Take that, Hawkins. I've got enough money to come through this shit. I'm solvent. I finish the second drink and sit the empty glass by a potted palm tree. My eyes are burning like a motherfucker. My hands itch. Fuck. I'm jumpy as shit. Maybe I should go. I could probably make it over to Tao's in less than half an hour if I could get a police escort.

I rub my eyes again. Okay, the cops probably wouldn't do that for me. Not unless I get in trouble. Maybe I should go find Hawkins and shove my fist into his tenth-grade-looking face again. Baby-faced motherfucker.

I cast my bleary gaze around the room. Crowded. Lots of important types here. The mayor and shit. Wonder where the hell Hunter is. I can't remember who's on our team. It's fucking hot in here. I'd love another blunt. Maybe I should go.

I fiddle with the gun and think about going to the bathroom and flushing it down the toilet. I don't need a gun. I've got my fists. Guns kill people—right? I don't want to do that. I'm a nice guy.

Can guns fit down toilets?

Right out in front of me, in between me and the tables they've got set up, this woman walks by, and she's a fucking fox. Short, blonde-brown hair. Angel face. Ass-hugging jeans. Maybe *that's* what I need to shake this weird-ass mood: a good fuck. I push myself up and start to follow her. If I ask, she might be game. I can donate some money to this charity bullshit. Stay in bed with her instead of playing.

I'm on her tail, my eyes glued to her pert little ass in those amazing blue jeans. Fucking hell. The way she moves…

There's Hunter! I see him in a crowd of well-dressed pricks, crossing through the room behind this one, angled toward me. I need to dodge him, follow the girl, but he holds his hand up. He raises his eyebrows—West's idea of a friendly greeting—then pulls his phone out of his tux pocket. He's getting a call, and whatever he hears makes his eyes go wide.

I turn back, and the girl is gone.

Goddamned Hunter. He's such a cock block.

I turn back toward the lobby, because I'm getting out of here. I don't have the right head for this Hearts bullshit.

I turn, and there's Hawkins.

"I DON'T KNOW what the fuck you want from me, but I told your asshat errand boy that I wouldn't have the money until Monday."

Hawkins, standing in front of me in a small, round sitting area off the rented casino room, smirks. "You didn't tell anyone shit."

"Monday," I growl.

Again, that smirk. "So make it Sunday, papa pimp." He grins and takes a step toward me.

I take a step forward, too, crowding him against the rounded wall. Wormy little bastard. I can take him with my eyes closed. "You gonna threaten me here, when you're all alone?" I sneer.

"I've got friends everywhere, Radcliffe."

"Good for you, you fucking prick. You'll get your money Monday. Now, you might want to consider getting the fuck away from me, before I get pissed off."

His face twists. "Sunday, or I'm coming for it."

"Why don't you try?" My self-control snaps and I shove him against the wall, enjoying the sensation of my hands digging into his shoulders. "I might owe you money, but you're a fuck-ing bully and a cheat. And getting the cops involved at Tao was— *hey!*"

I was going to say "a bitch move," but strong arms grab my shoulders from behind.

"Let's take this outside," Hawkins says, his beady eyes di-recting whoever is behind me. One of his thugs, obviously. I force my body to go limp as the man behind me pushes some-thing hard and cool into my lower back, and I'm shoved out a nearby door, into one of the casino's discreet atriums, with lush green grass, potted trees, and a bunch of cheesy lanterns.

Hawkins' thug digs his gun into my back, but I don't give a fuck. I whirl on him, kneeing him in the balls, sending him down to the plastic grass in half a second, before Hawkins' other goon throws a punch at my jaw.

I dodge it easily. My eyes are fast. One swift kick to the wrist, and his gun is on the ground. One more and that big, fat bastard is bleeding from his ugly fucking head.

I go for my own gun, rounding on Hawkins as I do—but my fingers aren't working right. I'm having trouble tracking. My mind is racing too damn fast now.

Goon No. 1 is back up, so I backhand the bastard and he flies across the grass. Another big bastard with that distinctive Hawkins Security swagger comes barreling out the door, and I kick him in the balls. Now they're all down.

But Hawkins has the gun, and he's circling me. "You high on something, Radcliffe?"

"Life."

He looks at me like I'm crazy, but he should have looked at me like I'm the fucking Flash, because I grab the gun from him and get him on the ground in half a second. I start wailing on his face, and it feels so good. Just what I need.

From somewhere far away, conscience tells me to lighten up—I'm gonna really hurt him—but I don't listen. I need this too badly.

I'm feeling better than I have in weeks when I hear a shriek, then feel small hands tugging at my shoulders. I aim a punch behind me and, a millisecond later, hear a woman's scream.

Holy fuck! I turn around, adrenaline pumping so hard I can feel my heartbeat in my eyes.

It's her. The blonde in the ass-hugging jeans.

I push Hawkins harder against the ground and search her face. Her cheek is red, like there's a bruise forming. "Jesus, baby. I'm sorry."

"You're going to kill him!" She backs away, scrambling like I'm some kind of monster.

And it fits—because I am.

Suri

THE FIRST THING I think: There's something wrong with him. The guy kicking ass in the tuxedo is too frenzied, too fast, too reckless.

He seems completely unafraid as he takes the big guys—obviously body guards—to the ground. The little guy has a gun, and just as I think I'm going to be witness to a murder, the guy in the tuxedo is on him, and the gun falls into the grass.

The little guy goes down like a rag doll, and Tuxedo Ass-Kicker drops on top of him and pounds his face with a gusto that's almost scary. Scratch that: It's *definitely* scary.

I press my back against the ivy-swathed brick wall that helps create the garden-like façade of the atrium. Blood is everywhere now; all over the thick green grass, coating Scrawny's face, staining Ass-Kicker's fists. I've never seen so much blood in all my life, not even the night Adam knocked my tooth out.

Finally, Scrawny's nose starts spraying—literally, spraying blood like a faucet. That makes my stomach lurch. It wakes me up. I fist my hands and lean forward. "Stop it!"

Ass-Kicker doesn't even flinch.

"Stop *right now*!"

I take a hesitant step toward them as my ears are filled with the awful sound of bone crunching. When Ass-Kicker doesn't respond, I rush up to him, throw my arms over his broad shoulders, and shriek right in his ear.

The hand that's punching Scrawny slings my way—lightning fast, before returning to Scrawny's face. A few of the knuckles catch me in the cheek hard enough to knock me off his back. I land in the grass, clutching my face as tears fill my eyes.

"Oh my God," I whisper as Ass-Kicker's gaze finds mine.

His eyes widen and his mouth drops open. "Jesus, baby. I'm sorry."

"You're going to kill him!" I scramble to my feet and run toward the door that leads back to the casino's hallway, but I've only taken a few steps when sirens start to wail. Not sirens like an ambulance, but sirens like an alarm system. I'm frozen midstep when a heavy arm locks around my waist. A deep voice purrs in my ear, "I'll show you the party."

The siren, accompanied by flashing red lights, is definitely of the security type. One of the cameras must have seen the fight.

Or me. I did run away from someone claiming to be a security guard, after all.

I tense, imagining scenarios as terrible as getting kidnapped or splashed across the inside pages of a tabloid, and the guy's grip on me gentles. "I'm a good guy. Swear."

Then he tugs me through the door, into the casino. I see a flash of light—red light, coming from chandeliers—and then I glimpse the security guard I escaped from. His dark eyes widen and his mouth pulls open into a snarl. "Ma'am—" he growls, and before he can get another word out, I am jerked in the opposite direction.

I'm moving because Ass-Kicker is pulling me. He's pushing me. He's bloody and he's gorgeous and he's trouble. I should run the opposite way, but Ass-Kicker seems to know where he's going—and I'm clueless.

We run through a few card parlors and down several crowded halls, up two sets of stairs and into a sleeker, quieter hall before he tugs me into a bathroom that looks more like a formal dressing room.

I'm not sure who drops whose hand, but suddenly I'm just standing there panting, in between a long, Victorian-style sofa pushed against one wall and a row of clam-shaped, white marble sinks topped with oversized mirrors on the opposite wall. The bathroom is empty, so my frantic breaths echo off the mahogany stalls.

I reach down to tug off one of my flats, which has given me a blister, and when I look back up, I find him slumped against one of the sinks, drained of that fierce animation that made him seem like a super-hero—or super-villain—just a minute ago. In fact, he looks tired enough to pass out. As I roll my gaze up and down his body, focusing for a moment on his familiar-looking face, his brown eyes rise to mine.

"You okay?" he asks, in that low, rough voice of his.

I frown, half because his voice is just so sexy; half because I'm not sure what he's referencing. He waves at his eye and it clicks. He hit me. Right.

I step to the sink beside him and look in the mirror, surprised to find there's not even a bruise. The area around my left cheek bone is a little puffy and a little red, but nothing to throw engagement rings about.

Still— "I must be crazy to have run in here with you."

He frowns, looking almost insulted. "What's wrong with me?"

"I just saw you try to beat some guy to death!"

He shrugs. "No, not to death." His eyes bore into mine. "He started it, too."

So he was defending himself. And enjoying it.

I should leave, because this guy is obviously, I don't know—I guess the only obvious thing is that he's bad news—but instead I lean my exhausted body against the sink. I'm sweaty and I'm still buzzed and still a little worried that the sirens going off were meant for me.

I don't think I did anything wrong, but clearly, security disagrees. The guard with the fuzzy eyebrows was hunting me. Unless he's not really a guard. What if he's *not* a guard? What if he's a kidnapper?

I take a deep breath.

Unlikely.

Just as I tell myself I'm going to make the rational decision and leave, my antihero straightens to his full, impressive height, strips his coat off, and tugs the pearly cuff links off his sleeves. He pushes them up, revealing thick forearms, and pumps some soap into one of his bloodstained palms.

I know his wrists and hands are red because he just kicked ass like a thug, but that doesn't prevent me being mesmerized by them. They're big and thick and slightly square, and they seem like competent hands. He's got them washed and dried on one of the casino's monogrammed towels within seconds, but after that his eyes flick up to the mirror, and I guess he notices at the same time I do that his crisp dress shirt is bloodstained, too.

He unbuttons it, and as I get the first peek at his deliciously ripped chest, I feel my cheeks color. I turn around to wash my hands as well. They don't need washing, but now that he's half undressed, I feel shy about walking past him to the door. Why have I stayed so long, anyway? Just to ogle him? How embarrassing.

I glance back over at him as I grab a towel, and I realize he really is beautiful: a living, breathing statue come to life. My eyes are drawn to his throat. It's thick and smooth and neatly shaven, in contrast to his lightly bearded face.

His face, I notice, looks kind of tight; his eyes troubled.

"Why'd you do that to that guy? I mean...how did it get started?

His mouth presses into a solemn line, then twists into a bitter scowl. "That guy's an ass. And *he* was the one who started it."

I almost laugh, because what he said sounds so eighth grade. Then he leans over the sink and splashes water up his arms and on his chest, and suddenly he seems much more adult.

I realize that I'm being obvious, but it's too late. He turns the sink off, wipes his arms and chest with a towel, and looks right at me.

Since I've already embarrassed myself, and I'm still kind of drunk, I steal one final glance at him, looking for tattoos or piercings: anything that gives even a little bit more info about who he is. At first I see nothing but his beautiful skin and well-honed body. Then I notice something dark along his side—a vertical scroll of text just over his hip.

I crane my neck a little, and the text jumps out at me: MARCH 15, 2007.

March 15 is the day I broke things off with Adam. I wonder what it means for him. Probably something sad. Why else would someone have a date tattooed on their body? Unless it's something good.

His eyes, when I look back up at them, seem slightly unfocused, but he doesn't seem to be on drugs or anything. Maybe he's a nice guy with a thousand friends. A nice guy just having a bad night. His suit looks bespoke and his shoes look like Berluti Derbys. He dresses like a guy who could even run in Hunter's circle. The thought rings a soft bell inside my fuzzy head, and suddenly I get the feeling that maybe I should know him…but that's impossible. Right?

My eyes gravitate to his rock solid pecs, but I jerk my gaze back up and frown at him. "Do you get in fights a lot?"

He rubs his forehead. "Only lately."

"You need to be more careful." That would be Mother Suri, who comes out at times of injury/sadness. He doesn't protest.

"I was careful." He pulls something small and metallic from his pocket and sets it in the sink. "Didn't use that, did I?"

My blood runs cold. "Oh my God, you had a *gun*?"

His brow tightens. "Lots of people have guns."

"I guess so." I look at the door, wondering how fast I can get out the door while at the same time trying to puzzle what it is about this guy.

It's a familiar feeling. Maybe I don't know him, but something about him feels very familiar. Or maybe it's simply how he makes me feel. He's clearly a mess, and that makes me feel needed. Kind of how I felt with Cross recently, as he's recuperating.

Who else was a mess? Adam.

I tilt my head a little, wondering if I've suddenly developed a fetish for men with issues. First, I was in a decade-long relationship with a guy who became an alcoholic—and a mean one, at that—and now I find myself getting hot for a guy who just got into a casino fight? Do I think I don't deserve a 'nice' guy?

But no.

I can tell right away that that's not it.

Adam was a nice guy, until he wasn't. And this guy…I want to lip-lock someone like this dude, a brawny badass, just so I can turn and walk away. So I can be the badass.

I could kiss him, I think. Take him by surprise and kiss him once, deep, and then ZIP out the door, and I'd be on his mind for the rest of the night.

I assess his face. It's a strong face—a sportsman's face—with a square jaw, a gladiator's nose, a short beard, and those deep brown eyes topped by strong brows. His hair is slightly messy, and it's hard to name a color: brown, blond, red?

He takes two steps closer to me, and I know I should probably hit the door and run from my weird, slutty impulse, but that chest. God, that chest is just amazing. It's freaking…Spartan. I'm shocked to find that I feel heavy, achy, damp between my legs. I tense my muscles there and the feeling spreads.

"You should go now," I tell him, but my voice cracks on the word "go."

This seems to catch his attention. He raises one brow. "You sure?"

I nod, and he turns away, toward the door. My eyes cling to his back—it's sleek, gym-ripped, and slightly tanned—and immediately, I feel a sinking sense of loss. This is a good thing, I start to tell myself.

And then he turns around. He grabs one arm of the couch and pushes it in front of the door, then turns to me. My mind fast-forwards. I can feel him stepping toward me before he even moves—and then he does. He *is*. He's within reaching distance, and his arms are going around me, pulling me to that chest, where I can feel the raw, pure heat of him.

"You're beautiful," he says, thumbing my short, highlighted hair out of my face. "I saw you earlier…walking down the hall. God…this ass." He squeezes it, bringing my hips flush with his strong thighs. I shut my eyes as his mouth covers mine, caressing then pulling away. His forehead touches mine, and he stares down at me.

"Your lips make me feel…well," he whispers, and as I'm wondering what exactly that means, he kisses me under my ear, along my neck, just where I've always liked it best.

His hands skate down my belly, playing with the waist of my jeans. Alarm bells peel in my head, but his mouth knows the code. I'm surprised to find my own hands pulling him closer.

"Oh, God." I want this, too. This…abandon.

His hands are in my shirt now, crawling up my belly, sneaking underneath my bra, gently skimming my breasts. I look into his face, opening my mouth to say I'm not sure what, but I find nothing but reverence in his features. Reverence and the kind of need that makes no sense, considering we've never even met.

His nimble fingers take care of my jeans button while his other hand continues stroking my breast. His hand is in my pants. I'm holding onto his hips. My eyes slip shut as his mouth worships my throat. He smells like shaving cream and…male.

"Not Adam," I whisper. *Or Cross.*

"No." He smiles, then lifts me up onto the nearest sink, where he spreads my legs, pushes my jeans down, and finds me underneath my lilac thong. His finger strokes me up and down. It feels amazing. I'm already wet.

"This is crazy," I gasp.

"I like crazy."

I guess New Suri does, too, because I let him finger me. While his deft hand makes me gasp, I hook my leg around his waist and pull him closer—close enough so I can rub him through the soft material of his slacks. He's hard and...huge. Like *whoa* huge. I can feel the head of him so well, even through his pants. I fold my hand around it, stroking down his length, and he's stretching his fingers inside me, and oh man, he's got the right spot. I am shaking, panting, clenching, coming apart to the sound of his low, wicked laugh. By the time I have the where-withal to look up into his brown eyes, I'm desperate to have him inside of me.

Then my hand around him pumps once more, and I watch his face tighten. He gives a low grunt, brown eyes closing, body slackening, and...

Oh my God! He's going to need another pair of slacks.

His eyes flutter open, and he laughs, low and quiet, almost like he's embarrassed.

I gawk at him. "Who *are* you?"

He grins, totally lazy, dominant male. "A guy with a pent-house. We can get to know each other better there."

I look down at myself, at my unbuttoned jeans, my still-trembling legs, my frisky hands—and I feel like Cinderella must have when the clock struck midnight. I meet his eyes—hypnotic eyes. "I- I can't go with you. I've got to find my friends." *And my purse*, I realize. Holy crap, I lost my bag! *That must be why I was getting chased!* My purse is so enormous...maybe they thought I was trying to leave a bomb or something. I probably looked even sketchier after I asked for Hunter. He's kind of a high-profile guy.

I slide off the sink, and my mystery man is there to catch me when my legs wobble. Looking at my face, into my eyes. Buttoning my jeans. I'm astonished when he sinks down to his knees and kisses me again, through my blue jeans.

"Beautiful woman." He grins up at me, then gets back to his feet. "Can I walk you somewhere?"

I look down at where he's laced his hand through mine. It feels...good. *Too* good, considering. I pull my fingers out of his and shake my head. "No. No—thank you."

I step toward the door, unable to tear my eyes away from him as he turns the sink on, splashing himself on his torso and lower on his pants legs to disguise the stain near his...

My face burns. I'm not some girl who messes around with strangers in casinos. I've never even had an orgasm from anyone else's hand but Adam's. Well, except my own.

Something about that thought brings tears to my eyes. The stranger is washing his hands again, drying them roughly with a monogrammed towel, and I realize I've missed so much in my time with Adam. We lost any semblance of spontaneity—any shred of lust or adoration—before we finished high school, and since then...since then we've just been drifting. *I'm* drifting.

The stranger's eyes find mine, and twin tears fall down my cheeks. I don't even know this guy, but I know I need someone like him. Someone who will make me *feel*. Someone who can't keep his hands off me.

This man, as his eyes hold mine...he seems to understand. He steps slowly to me, strokes my cheek. His eyes are so raw and real, I'm sure he sees right through me, down into the pitiful depths of my self-doubt. "There's nothing to feel bad about, okay?"

I nod—except I'm remembering what happened with Cross. The humiliating rebound attempt that probably wrecked our friendship.

Shameful tears fill my eyes as I shove the couch aside, then push through the bathroom door. Do I need affection so badly that I'll let myself get intimate in a casino bathroom?

I wipe my hand over my eyes, looking down at the glossy hallway floor and moving as quickly as I can when I hear someone say, "Suri!"

I jump as I slam into something, and there is Lizzy, dressed in skinny jeans, a giant beige sweater, and charcoal Chucks. She looks pink-cheeked and beautiful.

"Oh my God, Suri! Are you okay?"

I wipe my eyes and nod. "I lost my purse and security acted bizarre, and I didn't believe the guy was really security; I thought he was a kidnapper, so I ended up running off." I roll my eyes at myself. "It's a sad, pathetic story—" and that's not even telling half of it. I sigh softly. "Where were you when I called?"

"I'm so sorry, I fell asleep!"

Lizzy looks nervous, but before I can ask why, Hunter appears behind her, and he has my purse.

"Hunter. Thank you."

"The casino's director of resident operations said to tell you he's sorry about the misunderstanding. Whatever that means."

"I understand." I squeeze my eyes shut. I guess that's what I get for name-dropping.

I take the purse and Hunter frowns at Lizzy, then me.

Lizzy's face goes serious—that plastic, frozen kind of serious that always makes my blood run cold.

"Is something wrong?" I frown at Hunter, who's wearing a Lakers cap and a t-shirt. "I thought you had a fundraiser tonight..."

Lizzy turns to me and takes my hands, and my stomach clenches. "Suri, Cross is in the hospital—in El Paso."

"What?"

"You know how he was down in Mexico for that motorcycle convention? Well, apparently he got into another accident. But don't worry, it's not—"

"*Oh my God.* Is he okay?" My voice cracks, and tears fill my eyes so rapidly I can't see Lizzy's face.

"It's okay, Suri. A nurse called Love Inc. looking for Marchant, who isn't there, and when Rachelle didn't get

Marchant, she tried Hunter."

Liz nods at Hunter, who expounds. "The nurse said that he was fine, but being prepped for surgery."

"Another surgery?" My stomach clenches. "Then we need to go." I look around the hall as my mind shifts from nimble hands and warm lips to white hospital halls. "Let's go to El Paso now. I have my plane."

"Hunter's is already on the runway," Lizzy says. "I wanted us to be there when he woke up."

"Good idea."

She nods. "Your bags should already be on it."

Lizzy lightens the mood by telling ridiculous knock-knock jokes as we ride a shuttle from the back of the casino, past the palm-shaded golf course, toward the Wynn's VIP airport. I glimpse hangars as our path takes us over a small hill, and I'm amazed at how little I remember from when I landed…two hours ago?

"Suri."

"Hmm?"

"You're supposed to say, 'Boo who?'"

"Oh. Right." I shift my gaze from a W-shaped shrub to Lizzy's face. "Boo who?"

"Open the fucking door."

"What?"

Lizzy laughs. "'Who's there?' 'Boo.' You say, 'Boo who?' and I say, 'Open the fucking door.' It's funny. Remember humor?"

"I'm just so worried."

"Suri, he's okay. A *nurse* told Hunter he's okay. Nurses don't lie."

"I thought nurses couldn't reveal a person's medical condition."

"That's doctors."

"Oh."

The shuttle drops us off near the fence dividing the golf course from the airport—a fence I really don't remember going through at all—and I try to keep myself centered as I think about my mystery bathroom guy, and Cross, and my bathroom guy, and Cross, and how it'll be between us now, post-embarrassment. I guess he'll probably be normal. Maybe extra nice. It's me who's going to be awkward.

That low, deep voice rolls through my mind: *"There's nothing to feel bad about, okay?"*

He might have been a brawler and a bathroom slut, but my mystery guy was nice. I could tell.

I think of Adam at his book signing and feel a burst of anger. Adam sucks. Because he didn't really love me. Or rather, we weren't really *in* love. It took a dramatic act to help me figure that out. Is it because I wanted a happily ever after so badly I just overlooked all the signs?

Yes. And with Cross, I saw signs that weren't there.

We're approaching the twinkling landing strips, dotted with light-bathed control towers and those sleek, glass-looking hangers, when my mind starts playing tricks on me. Standing beside one of the planes, I think I see the guy from the bathroom.

I squint at him, because surely it's not the same guy, but as we get closer, I grow more certain.

My feet stop moving; Lizzy and Hunter take a few steps forward without noticing I've stopped. Lizzy is the first to turn around.

"Sur—you coming?"

"Who is that?" I whisper.

"Who, Marchant?" She jerks her thumb his way. "Radcliffe. I've talked about him before."

But I don't. I...can't. He can't— "He can't be Marchant."

My head spins and I grab onto Lizzy's forearm for support. I shake my head and look at him—the scoundrel's handsome face and scruffy beard. This can't be Marchant Radcliffe. Womanizing asshole. Pimp.

I just let him give me an orgasm.

CHAPTER FOUR

Suri

MARCHANT. MARCHANT RADCLIFFE. I keep blinking at him, because I can't believe my sexy bathroom guy is him: Marchant Radcliffe—the *pimp*.

We're close enough now that he lifts his head, and his gaze laps up and down my body in a manner I assume he must use with his harem. I feel heat rush into my face, followed by the sting of tears in my eyes, because he didn't understand me— back there when I was having my little freak-out. We didn't have a real moment. He's just good at this stuff. He's good at...well, at womanizing. He's a professional.

Lizzy grabs my hand, because my feet don't seem to want to take me to the plane, and we drop back as Hunter strides forward to greet Marchant.

"You okay?" she asks.

I nod—a little too frantically—and try to keep my wandering eyes off Marchant Radcliffe's bulky shoulders. We're less than twenty feet from the plane now, and as we get closer to the fold-out stairs, I can feel my body reacting—my skin warming, my heart rate speeding up—for a pimp, and it makes me feel like a fool.

I remind myself the attraction wasn't one-sided. The wet-spot still visible on his pants attests to that. I did nothing wrong. There's no reason I can't look him in the eye and act like an adult about this.

But what if he says something in front of Lizzy and Hunter? Then they'll *know*.

So what if they know?

It would change the way they think of me—that's what.

I'm Suri Dalton. Suri Dalton of the random-hook-ups-are-just-weird policy. I'm the one who discouraged Lizzy from selling her V-card at a brothel, because having sex is supposed to be meaningful.

Except it wasn't, was it? Having sex with Adam turned out not to feel so meaningful at all—at least in retrospect. So maybe I was wrong about what sex should be, but that doesn't mean I want Hunter and Lizzy to know about The Bathroom Incident. I had a personal moment, during which I felt like doing something outside my usual norm, and I'd like to keep that to myself.

Because you screwed around with a pimp.

I quiet the judging voice inside my head by insisting that it could have been any guy. Mr. Love Inc. was simply at the right place at the right time. It isn't as if I'm attracted to him in particular.

The guys are at the top of the stairs by the time Lizzy and I reach the bottom. By the time we step into the plane, they are, thankfully, out of sight. Hunter's flight attendant waves us past a curtain separating the cockpit from the cabin, and we step into a mod space done in black and gray and cream—the kind of space that screams 'I had this specially designed but didn't give the interior designer much creative leeway or any instructions.' There's not much of it, either: just a couch, a recliner, and a table, along with eight plush leather seats arranged in two rows of four along the right side of the plane. The rows face each other, like the benches of a restaurant booth.

When I don't see Hunter or Marchant at first glance, I allow myself to hope that maybe they've closed themselves into the plane's office. Then I realize that, unlike several of my dad's planes—the Boeing 767 and Gulfstream—this one doesn't look big enough to have an office.

Damn.

My hopes come crashing down when I spot them seated across from each other in the rearmost cluster of seats. Hunter's in a window seat, facing the front of the plane, with Marchant across from him in the seat beside the window seat. I divert my eyes from the back of that red-brown-blond head and am trying to decide if I can invent a reason to go into the plane's bedroom when Lizzy takes my elbow.

"C'mon, Suri. Let's sit down."

It's clear from Lizzy's distracted, slightly tired-seeming expression that she has no idea I'm tied in knots. If I run off now, she'll know for sure, and—my cheeks heat up—Marchant Radcliffe might tell them what happened.

Would he do that?

Of course he would! He's a pimp. Bragging about his sexual conquests is probably as natural to him as breathing air.

I gulp a big breath back, then paste a neutral expression on my face and smooth my blouse. I can do this. I can act natural. I need to get into that seat beside him and set a tone of normalcy. Strict normalcy.

As for his part, he's probably already forgotten me. Hoping that's true (and hoping it's not), I follow Lizzy with my head held high and my shoulders loose.

When we come into their space, Hunter's eyes sweep Liz like he wants to take her to the bedroom. In the moment they're eye-screwing each other, I brave my first glance at Marchant Radcliffe. He looks...different. And also the same. Now that I know who he is, I can see details I hadn't noticed before: like how he's wearing a flashy, platinum watch I'm pretty sure is IWC—the kind of timepiece that would be deemed totally excessive by a man like dad, but suits a brothel owner perfectly. His tux, originally nothing but a blood-spattered barrier to the body below, is in fact Brioni—the brand favored by James Bond. His light beard is impeccably trimmed, his mane of blond-brown-red hair impeccably cut, impeccably styled. Even his shoes look flawless—and that's *after* kicking someone's ass.

The boy-girl gods must be looking out for me, because while I ogle the pimp, he's looking down into a drink he's clutching. Something with orange juice—possibly a screwdriver?

I blink at him, waiting for him to look up. Waiting to set the tone between us. A jab of humiliated panic stings my chest, but I ignore it. When did I become so concerned about what other people think of me?

Lizzy takes a seat beside Hunter, and that's when Marchant snaps out of his daze. His eyes slide over me, and then he does a double take, his eyebrows shooting up into his hair.

"It's you," he says, in that soft, deep, sexy voice. My body reacts with goose bumps and a roller-coaster feeling in my stomach.

I give a little wave that is only slightly awkward and force my legs to lower me into the seat.

Lizzy's sharp blue eyes inspect the space between us. I can feel the curiosity oozing out her pores. She can tell that something's up. She's probably desperate to pounce on me, but she won't do it in front of Hunter and Marchant. Instead she presses her lips together and looks from me to Marchant, like a school teacher awaiting a pupil's answer.

I turn to Marchant— No, to Marchant *Radcliffe*. That's how I need to think of him. With some distance. I give him a smile I hope is generic. In doing so, I'm forced to look at his face. Kaa-pow! It's like bumping an electric fence. He's just so...handsome. The kind of handsome that's sturdy and square-jawed. Rugged. Like a cowboy. It's strange. He's supposed to be a pimp. Someone on the fringe of society. Someone weird. Perverse. Instead, he makes me think of Superbowls and sports cars. And sex.

I jerk my gaze away like he's a flame and I'm a wax girl. Edgy energy rips through me, making my fingertips shake; making my stomach feel empty. *Just ignore it.* I cross my legs at the ankle and set my purse on the floor beside my chair. By the time I'm looking up again, Lizzy's gone full-fledged detective. She's sitting up straighter in her seat and leaning forward, looking from me to Marchant like a bloodhound on a scent.

"I thought I knew the answer to this question, but...do you guys know each other?"

I open my mouth, but Marchant beats me to it. He grins at me. "I hit on her earlier, in the casino."

He gives me an exaggerated wink, and Hunter groans. "Leave her alone, man. Suri's not your kind of girl."

Except I am. Obviously I am his kind of girl. I just made out with him in the bathroom. More than made out. What is it we did? Second base? Third? I'm so out of practice, I don't even know.

I slide a glance at Marchant and find him swallowing back some of his screwdriver, wiggling his eyebrows conspiratorially. *Like something happened.* Damn.

I'm racking my mind for a change of subject when the intercom spits out static, and a deep, drawling voice lets us know we're preparing for takeoff.

"The flight to El Paso will take approximately one hour and forty-three minutes, guys and gals. Please fasten your seatbelts and leave 'em on until we are in the air and the fasten seatbelt light goes off."

I feel grateful that the intercom has helped the subject of Marchant Radcliffe and my acquaintance pass. Then he looks over at me and runs the tip of his tongue along his lower lip. His totally bitable lower lip.

My face heats up. My throat constricts. My eyes even water just a little.

This is nuts.

I glance first at Lizzy and Hunter to see if they notice my bout of temporary insanity. Both of them are looking at me. Looking at me like they *know*, or looking at me like I'm sitting right in front of them? I can't tell. I take a deep breath and look down at my feet.

Even from this angle, I'm tempted by the man whore next to me. His pants leg doesn't quite reach his slouching black sock, so I can see the barest swatch of thick, hair-dusted shin. Ridiculously, it heats me up.

Maybe that test was wrong. Maybe I *am* ovulating today. Clearly, my hormones are insane.

This guy owns a brothel, Suri. Where women—and men!—*sell their bodies. Do you approve of that?*

I actually shake my head as I argue with myself.

I think prostitution is disgusting. Damaging. And I think that whoever runs those sorts of shows is taking advantage of vulnerable women—and men.

An inconvenient memory flits through my mind: me, with my head thrown back and Marchant Radcliffe's hand down my pants. Me, wanting to mess around with a dangerous stranger because I thought it might give me a feeling of control. Me, making the choice to give myself away for *free*.

I could blame it on him. On his sex appeal. On that tux. I could say he tugged me into his orbit, because sex is his profession—but that would be a lie.

As the plane begins to taxi down the runway, I'm hyper aware of how much space he takes up in the seat beside me. His shoulders spill into my space, and I have to take a deep, measured breath to keep myself cool and collected.

The plane's wheels bounce off the runway for the final time, and we're airborne—just barely. Marchant sprawls his legs out in front of him, as if he's stretching. His left leg touches my right one. Heat spills through me. I dare not look down.

I blink straight ahead as Hunter pulls out an iPad and Lizzy pulls out a Kindle, and they lean their heads together, talking about how bright the screens are—or aren't. I catch a WTF widening of Lizzy's eyes at me, and I divert my eyes—to Marchant's leg, now pressed against mine.

I feel empty and achy in between my legs. I feel all tingly and weak. Sexed up…

Oh, God.

Using his Super Pimp powers, Marchant Radcliffe senses my moment of lust and goes in for the kill. He throws his arm around my shoulders, pulls me nearer to him, and rests his head on top of mine, inhaling. I can feel his hard, warm chest puff out. Can feel his face stroke my hair.

"Mmmm. You smell fucking good."

I'm frozen. A mouse being batted between a cat's paws.

He loosens his grip, and I can feel him looking down at me. "You're Trent Dalton's daughter."

I give a half nod without meeting his ridiculously pretty brown eyes, which he has pointed at me in some kind of Super Pimp seduction stare. "That's me."

"No one told me how fucking hot you are."

I force myself to look up at him, to meet his eyes. To keep breathing, even as my gaze retreats down to my lap.

I haven't been called "hot" since, I don't know, freshman year of college? But I'm blushing, and I'm pretty sure I wouldn't be if this was anyone but Marchant Radcliffe.

I swallow hard and flick my gaze to him. "No one told me *you* had such bad language."

He laughs and gulps back some of his drink. When he moves the glass away from his face, I'm struck again by his sheer male radiance. "You don't use 'swear' words?" He makes air marks around swear, and says it in a meek, little old woman type of voice.

"I use them when they're warranted," I say, trying not to laugh at his voice.

"You *are* fucking hot. It's warranted."

I take a deep breath. "You come on strong," I say, and I'm proud of how dry my voice sounds—like I don't care one bit.

"That's what they tell me." He's proud. I'm sure coming on strong has gotten him into a million pairs of blue jeans. But I don't like guys who come on strong—do I?

With one arm still around me, Marchant Radcliffe reaches into the magazine rack, pulling out a smallish bottle of Grey Goose I guess he had hidden, and adds a few inches to his drink. Then he offers it to me.

"You look like you could use a little liquid R&R."

As he says it, he presses his leg against mine again.

Butterflies shoot through my stomach. I move my leg. Shake my head.

"I'm fine. Maybe a little tired." Because I already got smashed once today, I think as I direct my gaze to the curved ceiling. *Because I'm losing my damn mind.*

He takes another long swig of his drink, and just when I've almost managed to peg him as a stereotype—rollicking frat boy/man whore in grown-up clothes—he grabs my hand and shuts his eyes.

"I know you're gonna pull it away, but could you just give me a minute? Kinda helps…ground me."

My hand twitches around his and I find myself staring at his eyelids. "You don't like to fly?"

"That's the short version," he mumbles.

"I assumed you'd be in the jet set."

He flips his eyes open, and they look dark. Just…weirdly dark. "I don't want my own plane."

I get an odd feeling in my chest, like he's telling me something more personal than he doesn't like to fly. I flip through my mental list of celebrities, politicians, and business people who've been in plane crashes or near-crashes, but I don't remember Marchant Radcliffe being among them. And then I remember: his parents died in a plane crash.

I stare at my knees, because I'm not sure how to respond to him, and I'm surprised to feel his hand stroke down my neck. It feels good. Tickles. He leans in closer, brushing my fingers with his and resting his head on my shoulder.

It's easy to pretend that this is the kind of passion I've been looking for. Then I peek my eyes open and notice Lizzy and Hunter have looked up from Hunter's iPad and are staring.

I tug my leg away from his, attempt to shrink away from him even though his arm is still around me. "I'm not your type, remember?"

"I know that." He's nuzzling my neck.

Lizzy and Hunter get up abruptly, heading toward the bedroom just a bit too quickly, and Marchant and I are left alone. His arm is still around me, and I'm forced to face the fact that I like it.

"Is this an every woman thing, or just me?" I whisper—because despite myself, I have to know. "Are you just someone who likes to toy with people?"

He pulls away, and it's like a house of cards falling. His eyes are surprisingly bleak when he says, "It's a 'me thing,' Suri Dalton." He laughs, humorless. "I've…I don't know. I've got problems."

As I move from my seat to one across from him, desperate to put some space between us, I decide it's a *me* thing, too. Because even as he takes a long swig straight from his bottle, I can't seem to get my body to calm down.

Marchant

GODDAMN. THIS IS gonna happen here, and when it does, this beautiful angel is gonna see it.

I stand up, bottle in my hand, but there's nowhere to go. The bedroom door is closed, and most of the cabin is this open fucking room.

I pace toward the cockpit and my mind is filled with crazy shit. I duck behind the curtain and I breathe into my elbow.

Calm down, fuckhead. You just gotta make it till we land.

I twist the cap off the Goose and pour it down my throat.

"Mr. Radcliffe?"

I blink at the flight attendant who just appeared in front of me. I can't remember her name right now, although I'm aware that I should know it. She touches my arm, and I'm tempted to slap her.

"Can I get you anything?"

I move away and shake my head, already drifting back into the cabin.

Standing here, looking at the back of Suri Dalton's hair, I feel like I'm stuck in a movie I can't turn off. I feel like the only way out is to open the door and just…jump.

That's crazy.

Fuck me.

I sink into the recliner and take a deep pull of my vodka. Put one arm over my head. I try to pretend I'm in my garden house.

I swallow—the sound of it is so loud—and open my eyes, so my eyelashes brush the leather of the chair's arm. For a moment, my body is completely immobile. As I imagine her arms around me. As I think of what I'd like to do to her throat. To her breasts. As I return to the image of her arms around me. It'd feel good to be hugged. Held.

And then I hear her coming up on me. I hear her soft voice, asking, "Are you okay?"

Without lifting my head, I say, "I'm fine. I'm just fucking drunk. Started drinking…way too early."

I wish that was really the problem.

CHAPTER FIVE

Suri

SO MAYBE MY first instinct, back there in the atrium, was right. Maybe something *is* wrong with this guy. And it's not that he's a pimp, and it's not that he's a player. I think Marchant Radcliffe must have an alcohol problem.

Clearly, the universe has decided my adventure into bad-boy land has lasted long enough, and offered me a solid reason to stay away from him. And I'm grateful for that. I tell myself I'm grateful for it as I watch him stride into the big, steel elevator on the first floor of El Paso's University Hospital.

I'm trying to think of it like...I don't know...a muffin. A really good blueberry muffin—my favorite kind of muffin. Except this muffin got dropped in dirt. Or kitty litter! Yep. You wouldn't want a blueberry muffin dropped in kitty litter, no matter how good a muffin it was. No matter how delicious it looked from far away. Because eating a muffin dropped in kitty litter would be like asking to get sick.

So as my eyes dart over his handsome face and his impressive body—a body just as scrumptious as any blueberry muffin—I remind myself that he's a drunk. At least I think he might be. It's a definite possibility.

Also possible: He got drunk because he's scared of planes.

Because his parents died on a plane. I wish I knew more about that. I wish I could ask Lizzy about it.

Since she and Hunter came out of the bedroom, right before we landed, I haven't been able to get her to look me in the eye. I'm not sure what's with her sketchy behavior, but the bitchy prude inside me says she knows something happened between Marchant and me, and she respects me less for it.

I keep my gaze on my feet again as the elevator lifts us to the third floor. I think of Cross. I think of how I wasn't thinking of Cross on the plane ride over. I'm a pretty shitty friend.

I think, again, of putting the moves on Cross. What was that all about? I've tried hard to self-analyze, but I'm honestly not sure. Not completely. I'm not in love with Cross. I know that. I love him the same way I love Lizzy, except he's also an attractive and charming guy.

I guess...I don't know. I hate to be one of those people who excuse themselves by saying things like, "I just wasn't in a good place," but that's what it comes down to, I guess. That and I was just dumb dumb dumb.

The elevator door opens, cutting off my thoughts, and putting us off inside a wide, white hallway. Anxiety spreads through me, because I remember this from last time—from Cross's motorcycle accident back in November—and I really don't want to remember that.

A lump tightens in my throat as I wonder if this will be like that. Memories toss themselves into my consciousness like a stack of Polaroids thrown into the air: Cross, bleeding, swollen, bandaged. That horrible breathing tube. The catheter bag. I remember talking to Adam on my cell phone from the waiting room while Cross endured his first long surgery, just a few hours after the crash, and my stomach twists.

I'm in the back of the group, so I allow a tear to slip out of my eye as I breathe the acrid scent of rubbing alcohol, lemon disinfectant, and rubber. We walk a few dozen more feet to a big, half-circle desk., "OR Waiting Room" is written above the desk in stainless steel letters.

One of the people behind the desk—a slim, short man wearing light brown scrubs—glances up at us. "Can I help you?"

Lizzy pulls her wallet out of her purse and wiggles an ID out of one of its pockets. It's a fake that says Elizabeth Carlson—one she had made so she could visit Cross in the ICU after his first accident. She slides it across the table. "We're here for Cross Carlson."

The man behind the desk looks into her face, a blend of curiosity and pity. "Are you the wife?"

"Sister," she says softly, and Hunter takes her hand.

The man's blue eyes meet Lizzy's. "Maybe you can help us. We haven't been able to find Ms. Carlson."

"Ms. Carlson?"

The man nods, frowning. "Meredith Carlson?"

I clutch my purse as the room tilts around me, and the man in scrubs explains that Cross arrived with his wife. I tell myself he must be wrong—the man is obviously wrong.

"She was very upset," he tells us.

Lizzy straightens her shoulders, and explains, in her most gathered, Lizzy voice: "I think there's a misunderstanding. My brother isn't married."

The man behind the desk shrugs. "Could have fooled me."

I stare at Lizzy's shoulders, and Hunter starts asking questions like how long until we'll get an update, and is Cross still in surgery, and the man in brown scrubs tells us yes; the surgeon will be out to speak to us soon.

"Is he okay?" I hear myself ask as the others head for little plastic seats.

"He's in surgery, ma'am."

"But he's...okay? Like...when they brought him in, he was doing pretty well?"

"They took him back to surgery," the man says. "That's all I know."

"Did you see him?" The man's neutral expression begins to slip, and I add, "I'm just trying to find out all the information I can."

"Well, he can't tell you."

I turn to find Marchant Radcliffe standing right behind me. He has one eyebrow arched and both arms crossed. For some reason, the stern, knowing look on his handsome face pisses me off.

"This is none of your business." I look into his blood-shot eyes. Eyes that are blood-shot because he's drunk.

He blinks. "You want to tell me my business?"

Heat crawls over my skin at the challenging tone. The same kind of challenge Adam used to issue when he'd been drinking. I hold my head up higher. "I'm not doing that. I'm telling you what your business is *not*. My concern for my friend is *not* your business. Not unless you have something helpful to say." I nod at the chairs behind him. "You can go and sit back down now."

His eyes, on mine, feel hot. "You want me to leave?"

"Did I say that?"

"Do you?"

"I don't care if you leave or not." My voice wavers, because I'm upset about being in a hospital again, and now Marchant Radcliffe has turned Adam on me. I whirl away from him, headed toward where Lizzy and Hunter are sitting, when another set of wide steel doors opens and a man wearing pale blue scrubs, a little blue hat, and black sneakers strides out.

He looks around the room, gaze swinging first to me and then to Lizzy. "Meredith Carlson?"

I close the distance between us, my stomach twisting into a sick knot as I note a few blood smears on his scrubs. My heart is beating so hard I can barely speak, and when I do, my voice sounds low and thick. "Is he okay?"

The doctor—a man about my father's age—blinks his pale

brown eyes. "Are you Meredith Carlson?"

"I'm— no. I'm not. He doesn't have a wife."

The surgeon's thin brows notch, his eyes darting around the room as if he's already dismissed me. "I was told he has a wife." His eyes search the space behind me, and Lizzy steps into my peripheral vision with her hand extended. "I'm Lizzy. I'm his sister."

"I'm Dr. Hilcox." The doctor's hand clasps hers, and he gives her a little nod. "Your brother came through the surgery just fine. He had a bullet wound to the shoulder and a fractured ankle. I also cleaned an older wound—his hand." The man's lips draw up, like he's about to tell us something unpleasant, and my pulse skyrockets. "During the procedure, he asked repeatedly for Meredith. I understand he's had some injuries recently. Perhaps some emotional trauma, from being back inside a hospital. In the recovery room after his surgery, he got quite worked up. We had to increase his sedation."

"He was asking for someone named Meredith?" Lizzy frowns.

The surgeon nods, looking from me to Lizzy, like he simply can't believe neither of us is named 'Meredith'. He shrugs, looking around the waiting room once more before telling us Cross should be settled in the ICU in twenty or thirty minutes, and we'll be able to visit him one at a time. "Wait here or in the ICU waiting room. A nurse will let you know when it's time."

"The ICU?" I speak before I think about it, and the surgeon's eyes snap onto mine.

"Yes. The ICU."

"But I thought he…" I shake my head, feeling dizzy and disoriented. "I thought it wasn't serious. The nurse said…"

"What nurse?" the doctor asks. He looks peeved. Like he's in a hurry and I'm keeping him from something.

"The nurse who called. She said he wasn't hurt badly."

The surgeon's eyes narrow. "Our nurses don't make phone

calls about patients. Can you tell me what you're talking about?"

I frown. I'm feeling...frozen. Like I'm in a state of shock. "He's really in the ICU? I just...I haven't even been worrying." God. I feel like such an awful friend.

All I can think about is how Cross would feel about being back inside an ICU. I was with him so often after he woke up from his coma. Cross and I. Just Cross and I. He told me things he hadn't told anyone...and...God, it breaks my heart to think he's here again. Inside another hospital. Recovering again.

I bite my lip and turn away. Lizzy and Hunter keep talking to the doctor, but I need to find somewhere to collect myself. I notice Marchant noticing me, and he acts like he's going to break away from the discussion to check on me.

No thank you.

I take off down the nearest hall I see. My emotions are like clothes being tossed around a dryer. I can't tell up from down. All I know is that I'm hurt, and I don't want to see Marchant Radcliffe or anyone else right now.

He follows me. Of course he does. I pick up my pace, till I'm practically running past doors and carts and metal structures like wine racks but laden with oxygen tanks, past a nurse wearing mint green scrubs when I can feel him closing in on me.

"Suri Dalton, slow the fuck down!"

I toss a blurry glance back over my shoulder. "Don't curse at me! And go away!"

I don't know why I'm so upset. I just can't synthesize it. Then I remember—they said Cross was married—and it's like something bursts open inside my chest, and I'm directionless and dizzy and distraught, and I realize what I've wanted this whole time: to be settled. I knew I wanted that, of course, but I didn't know how much until right now. I think of Cross's strong, stable arms around another woman and I feel like something is clawing at my heart.

Why don't I have that?

Why didn't he want me?

Why didn't Adam care enough about me to change?

For a moment, I almost forget I've got Marchant Radcliffe on my heels. Then I can't forget, because he's right there on me, grabbing my arm.

I push away from him, and he pushes me up against the wall. His arms touch down on either side of me, pinning me in. His hand goes into my hair and I can feel him breathing, smell him breathing. Smell the vodka.

"Jesus, woman. You can move."

I react irrationally, because in the moment, I'm grieving. Not just for the loss of any chance I might have wanted with Cross, but for the loss of what I thought I had with Adam.

I miss being coupled! I miss snuggling up to a warm body in bed. I miss being known. Being accepted and loved.

I blink at the beautiful man in front of me, and I push against his chest as I start to cry. "Go away," I sob. "I'm upset!"

His mouth is on my neck so fast, I don't know what hit me. "That's exactly why—" he says as he bites me— "I'm not leaving you alone."

He kisses me, and I kiss him back. My hands are all over him, grabbing at his hips, pulling him into me. He grabs my breasts, my ass. His hand moves to my back, where his fingers dig so hard they almost hurt.

As he looks at me, his eyes grow stormy. Just like Adam's used to. "You his girlfriend, Dalton?"

"What are you talking about?"

"Are you Carlson's girlfriend?"

"Why?"

"Are you?" He looks pissed off.

"No."

"You wish you were?"

"That's not your business."

"Everything about you is my business."

"You're crazy."

"And you've got a thing for Carlson."

"No I don't. We're just friends." But I sound guilty.

His face goes from furious to disdainful in a second. He looks me up and down—scornful in his assessment. And like before, in the bathroom at the Wynn, I feel as if he can see every part of me I don't like. His eyes return to mine, heavy with the verdict of his judgment. "I had pegged you for lonely and inexperienced, Dalton. Not desperate."

I'm pretty sure my mouth falls open, because I'm shocked. Not just by the meanness of his comment—although it is definitely mean—but because it snags me like an arrow in between the ribs. Because it's true. I'm both lonely and desperate. How did I get here? I blink at him, and the hall around me seems to tilt.

"You're an asshole," I whisper.

He glares, a smirking, petulant look that reminds me slightly of a child. *Or a drunk.* I close my eyes. He's just like Adam. Nice guy, sober. Mean drunk. I'm single for mere weeks and the first guy who catches my eye is a mean drunk!

My eyes tear up again, and I think it's probably good that I'm infertile—a failsafe, because apparently the only men I'm going to end up with are assholes.

I rub my eyes and get a blurry glimpse of Marchant Radcliffe. He looks serious. Almost solemn. "You're right," he says. "I am an asshole. Crippled Carlson's probably a better choice."

He shrugs, then stalks toward the elevators, and this time I know my mouth is hanging open.

CHAPTER SIX

Suri

I VEER DOWN a different hallway, wrapping my hand around my blouse and jerking hard as I let out a furious sob.

I look down to find my bra showing. It's lacy and beige, and I don't know when anyone will see it again. This makes me cry harder. And then I pass a man in scrubs and I realize...I'm half naked!

"Damnit." I look up and down the hall. A dozen or so yards ahead of me, a group of people in scrubs rounds a corner. They look young. Like...my age. Interns? Residents?

I clamp my hand over my mouth and try the first door I see. It's unlocked, so I rush inside. I blink at some metal supply shelves through blurry eyes and try to hold back my tears so the people passing by in the hallway won't hear me crying like a lunatic. Then I see the woman standing in front of me and I'm so shocked I start to sob again.

Everything is so messed up...

I don't plan to sit down; my legs wobble, and suddenly I'm sitting cross-legged on the cold tile floor, holding my head because I'm freaking out. And I'm not thinking about Marchant Radcliffe, the world's biggest dick. I'm thinking about Cross. Who might be *married*. Cross who I tried and failed to seduce.

Cross who I could have loved. Could have built a life with.

I mean, yes, he's a player sometimes. Yes, he gets drunk and horny and seduces twins with names like Barbie and Cookie. But he's a good guy, and he's my friend. And suddenly, I want him more than anything. But he doesn't want me.

I fold a hand over my head. "What's wrong with me? What's wrong with ME?!" My eyes fly to the woman in the closet with me.

She's got wild red hair and big green eyes, and I can't stand the weight of her curious gaze so I jump up. "I don't understand what's wrong with me!"

She's about my age, and she looks like she thinks I just escaped the psych ward. I'm crying as I watch her gather herself. I can practically see her trying to decide what to say as she looks me over. I press my lips together to try to stop my crying, and she settles on: "What happened to your shirt?"

That sets off another wave of sobs. I look at the girl through my tears, and she looks at me. She looks freaked out. I don't blame her. I rub my hand over my face and say, "I tore it."

She looks at me like she's wondering how that happened, and I shake my head. "No, I'm saying I tore it. I got pissed off and tore it, like a wrestler!"

The woman laughs. I laugh, too. "It's okay. I'm insane. I know."

"You're not insane. Just upset," she says kindly. And I notice that her red hair is wild. Like she's been on an adventure. Maybe she has. Maybe she would understand if I told her.

"My life is so messed up. You don't even know. First my fiancé broke things off and then I fell for my best guy friend. It was messed up—really messed up—but I've had a crush on him since like, the dawn of time, and he was in the middle of a really awful time and I just…I don't know." Tears clog my throat. "I think I just wanted to be invaluable to someone." I meet the woman's green eyes and hold her gaze, pretending I am in confession. "He really needed me at the time, and I wanted to feel special. I let myself get carried away, and then I embarrassed myself. And now he's here, and I want to be his friend and be here for him but I'm not sure how I can."

I wipe my tears, then glance around the room, suddenly remembering I'm in a supply closet. I inspect the little room more closely and notice a black leather jacket folded neatly on one of the shelves. A familiar black jacket. "Oh my God, is that Cross Carlson's jacket? Are you his wife? Are you that biker chick he met in Mexico?"

Her eyes bug out, and oh my God. I whirl around. "I can't believe I told you all that! I can't—Oh my God!"

Well this settles it: I will never, ever let myself fall for the wrong person, ever again. Not a friend and not a drunk. In fact, I refuse to fall for any guy!

Marchant

I BUMP INTO Missy King on the first floor of the hospital. It's maybe half an hour after I was an asshole to Suri, after I've arranged to have a private plane take me home.

Missy King is this call girl type who used to be friends with some of the women at my ranch. She vanished two years ago, and everyone assumed she was dead.

So I'm surprised to see her.

At first, I just stare at her, wondering if it's really her, or if my addled mind is playing tricks on me. But she continues to be there, petite, red-haired, looking much the same (one of the things my mind is actually good at is remembering faces). Then, she seems to notice me. Yep, she thinks I'm familiar. So I walk into the little seating area where I spotted her and decide to offer my services as Rescuer, pro bono.

"I don't know what you're doing," I say after I walk up to her, "if you're safe or not, but I can keep you safe," I promise. "You can hide out at the ranch—as long as you want. No strings."

I say other things. Maybe they're more eloquent. It's interesting how I can be in my head and say whatever I'm saying to convince Missy King to come with me, and I'm not really aware of the words.

If she notices that I'm a few colors short of a rainbow right now, she doesn't show it. The taxi ride is quiet, and when we reach the private airport where the plane is waiting, she follows me up the stairs without asking any questions.

I'm not inclined to try to talk to her. I've made enough of an ass of myself today without adding to it, and she doesn't seem interested in talking anyway.

Before the plane takes off, I lock myself inside the little bedroom and stare at the ceiling while I battle my demons. The same ones I've always had. The ones I know I can't afford to listen to. I put my hands over my ears. I roll over on my stomach. I dig my fingers into my hair. I cup the tattoo on my side and try to pretend it isn't there. I get up and pace the bedroom.

I step out of the room for a minute and watch Missy, working a crossword or Sudoku or some shit. She looks okay. She's still here, so I figure she's not a hallucination. I've been known to hallucinate when I'm in this state.

I shut myself back into the tiny bedroom and allow my mind to wander to Hawkins. How much I'd like to kick his ass again. But when the plane lands at the airport behind the Love Inc. ranch, I'm shaking and I just need to find someone to fuck.

I call Rachelle and tell her to put Missy in my suite at the main house. I also tell her to put one of the guards outside her room.

"We'll talk about this tomorrow," I say before I end the call, even though I know I won't be any better tomorrow.

After aiming Missy—Meredith, she said her real name is— toward the main house, I hurry around the pond, to my garden house, and slam the door. I feel a little more relaxed, but I'm still geared up. My clothes feel itchy, so I peel them off and throw on a robe.

Then I call Ansley's, a discreet escort service I used to use, years ago, before I decided it was bad for business. I order three women, all with short, dark hair, and spend the next few hours trying to escape myself.

When they leave, I stumble into the bathroom, dressed in nothing. I look at myself in the mirror and I see someone I've never seen before. I try to pull the wrong hair out and try to wash the wrong face off, but it doesn't work. In fact, I'm bleeding now.

From somewhere very far away, I remember Dr. Libby telling me to take some Ativan if this happens. So I take some. I can't remember how many, so I settle on five, and now it's getting dark.

CHAPTER SEVEN

Suri

I STARE OUT the floor-to-ceiling window that serves as one of my small bedroom's four walls. The view is post-card pretty. Dusky, golden light twinkles off a large, heart-shaped pool. All around the pool are iron chairs and ferns. Behind that, shadowed by the setting sun, is a grove of oak trees so large I can hardly see their tops. Through the shadows, past a few weeping willows and a beautiful pond, are two rows of cottages. English-style, so stone, with wooden shingle roofs and lots of wildflowers all around the front porches.

I feel like I'm at a resort, but that's just a façade. Because this isn't a resort, and I can't really enjoy these beautiful grounds. In fact, I haven't enjoyed myself since we arrived yesterday afternoon.

That's because the resort is Love Inc.

Marchant Radcliffe's brothel.

Cross is recovering, aided by the open bar in the first floor lobby. We came here for him—so Lizzy and I could keep an eye on him while he recovers from the loss of "Merri"—but so far, the place doesn't seem to be helping him at all, and neither are we.

Meredith is the real name of Missy King, one of Cross's father's former mistresses—one who got caught up in a terrible situation and ended up sold as a sex slave in Mexico.

I'm still not clear on all the details, but somehow Cross found out about her fate and went south to try to find her. He did, but after they made it to America, she disappeared again.

He isn't actually married to her. That was just a lie they told at the hospital.

The weird thing is, I'm pretty sure Cross wishes it was true.

I don't know for sure, because he won't talk to me. He won't talk to anybody. He'll hardly even come out of his room on the second floor. If Lizzy and I want to see how he's doing, we have to knock for ages before he *might* open the door—and if he does, he's red-eyed and solemn. Like he's mourning for this woman. Which I guess he is. Clearly, he is.

I watch some uniformed employees pull a sheet of cement over the pool—they seem to be turning it into a dance floor—and wish the Cross thing didn't bother me. I shouldn't care that Cross has fallen hard for this girl. It's not my business, and besides, no one even knows where she is. I hope she's okay, and I *should* hope she pops back up, but if I'm totally honest with myself, I hope she stays away. I don't know much about her other than her unfortunate situation in Mexico, but…at one point she was seeing Cross's father. That's just sleazy—right?

Why doesn't Cross think so?

I lean my head against the window and sigh. My breath makes a fog circle on the glass, obscuring the backyard, so all I can see is the fading gold of sunlight and a bunch of shadows. It suits my mood.

Somehow, I got stuck with Lizzy and Hunter in this huge suite Marchant built for Hunter back when this place first opened and the boys were living out their frat house fantasy.

The suite is large enough for three, I guess—it has four bedrooms—but it's still awkward, sharing space with them. I feel like a third wheel.

This is made worse because I *know* Lizzy is keeping something from me. I'm not sure what, but she never hangs around to talk to me when Hunter goes into the Love Inc. library to work. She grabs her laptop and says she's going off somewhere in the building to work herself, on her master's thesis; she's trying to complete it at a distance, and I get that…but it's weird that she doesn't want to spend *any* time with me. We're best friends, remember?

My breath on the window dissipates, and I see a cluster of beautiful women spill around the pool. They're talking animatedly about something—I can hear their voices through the glass—and my heart catches when I realize the woman at the center of the group is Lizzy.

I swallow hard and tell myself to grow a thicker skin. She's doing her ethics thesis on the escorts here, so of course she needs to talk to them. Besides, they're her friends now—right?

She introduced me to most of them almost as soon as we arrived here. And when we came back to the room, I was withdrawn and quiet because I feel kind of uncomfortable around these confident, extroverted women who see things so differently than I do.

Lizzy knows me. She could probably tell I was uncomfortable, so she's hanging out with them solo. What's the point of inviting me?

I sit back on my king-sized bed and think of Cross, occupying the single room nearest to the stairs, one floor up.

I could check on Cross.

I will check on Cross. He's probably in his room brooding. But he's the reason I'm here, after all. And if he doesn't answer the door, I'll go do some yoga by the pond.

I dress in black yoga pants and a pink sleeveless shirt, plus my sneakers, and I'm out the door in just a few minutes.

I knock twice on Cross's door before he answers. My heart jumps into my throat. He hasn't answered my knocks since we've been here. All I want is for our friendship to go back to normal. The door swings open, and I find myself staring at a young, strawberry-haired girl.

I frown. "Meredith?"

She shakes her head. "Lucy. I'm cleaning up."

"Oh, so Cross is gone?"

"I guess so. The room is empty."

It smells like a bar. I feel sorry for the girl. "Okay...well, thanks."

She nods and closes the door, and I'm not sure what to do with myself now. I make a slow circle on a red runner covering the hardwood. There's another one of those big, floor-to-ceiling windows at the end of the hall. I can see Lizzy by the pool with her escort friends. I tell myself I could be out there with her, if I hadn't acted so reserved—okay, antisocial—last night.

I can't help remembering the conversation Lizzy and I had before she came to Vegas: me, telling her that sex should be with someone you really care about, and Lizzy insisting that it didn't have to matter so much. Now Lizzy's met her soul mate and I'm alone, letting drunk strangers get me off in bathrooms, no less.

How the tables have turned...

Maybe what bothers me most is that every other second I'm here, I'm thinking about Marchant Radcliffe. It's not what he said or how he behaved that's the problem. It's that he caught my eye at all. Because that's what enabled him to hurt me with that nasty comment in the hospital hall. I let him in. I, Suri Dalton, am addicted to drunken assholes.

I rub my eyes and head back downstairs, where I plan to take a side door and an indirect route to the pond. As I walk, I keep my eyes peeled for Marchant Radcliffe, while my mind regurgitates the scene from the Wynn bathroom.

The old Suri would never do something like that. She had pride. And poise.

"I had pegged you for lonely, not desperate..."

I bite my lip.

I head through the main hall, a massive, rug-covered area filled with bookshelves, couches, and cozy alcoves where the women and men who work here meet their clients, before then taking them back to their rooms. I hurry past the open bar and past the elevator shaft, headed for a door that's topped with a glowing, red EXIT sign on what I think is the side of the building.

I'm bursting through the door, already feeling the soft heat of the night on my cheeks, when someone yelps.

I take a big step back and find myself staring at a red-haired woman. She's petite, with huge breasts, an hourglass waistline, and a fine-boned face. She has twinkling green eyes, traces of dimples on either side of her mouth, and she's wearing an elegant, green wraparound dress. Obviously an escort.

"I'm so sorry," she says, stepping back, onto a little garden path.

"That's okay. It was probably my fault." I stare at her face for a second before my hands fly to my mouth. "Oh my God, I know you! You're that nurse! You're an escort, too?"

It's rude to blurt it out this way, but my mouth moves before my brain can stop it.

And then, while her face twists and her mouth opens wordlessly, my brain makes a furious lunge forward.

This woman has red hair.

Lizzy told me 'Meredith' has red hair.

"Oh my *God. You're Missy King!*"

"Meredith," she whispers, wide-eyed.

"Wow." So this is her: Cross's Meredith. My gaze sweeps her small, taut body, and I can't help comparing myself to her. Cross didn't even want to kiss me, and he wants to marry her. As my eyes sweep her body, she takes a wobbly step back. She's about to turn, to go, but all I can think about is the one glimpse I've had of Cross today, late this morning when Lizzy pried the door open and I peeked in: Cross, lying in his room, propped up on pillows, sipping something alcoholic and playing solitaire on his phone. "Have you seen Cross yet?"

She bites her lip, and I forge ahead—for Cross's sake. "He misses you so much. And yeah, if you were wondering, I'm okay with that." My failed attempt at seducing Cross came up when I babbled to the "nurse" in the supply closet, so I'm sure she thinks I'm in love with her man. "Cross is one of my very best friends, and I just want him to be happy. I think he would be, if he knew that you were here. Does he know?"

She steps back a little more. "I haven't talked to him."

"So...are you?"

Her green eyes meet mine, and my heart sinks before she opens her mouth. "Listen...I'm just laying low here for a while. Until I get my life together again. It has nothing to do with Cross. I didn't even know that he would be here."

"Do you care about him?" I ask bluntly.

Her eyes burn. "I care very much about him, but there's lots of baggage between us. Lots of...obligation." Her mouth twists downward.

"Well I can tell you this. He really seems to care about you, and I'm sure you know, he's been through a lot. Be careful with him, okay?"

She nods, tears filling her eyes, and dashes off between the trees, toward what I'm pretty sure is the escorts' dormitory.

My stomach is in knots as I walk the other way, into the bushes I hope will hide me from Lizzy and everyone at the pool.

I've heard there's a large, shrubbery maze to the left of the pond, before you reach the cottages. It's a unique feature, so I tell myself my aimless nighttime walk has an educational purpose. That I'm not just running from my troubles.

I breathe deeply as I move under massive weeping willows and between carefully manicured snap roses. Despite the turmoil in my heart, I can't help but feel impressed. This place might be a cesspool of sex-for-pay, but the grounds and the interior design are stunning. I tell myself they have to be, to keep the clients coming—har de har—but I can't help wondering if the lavish grounds say more about Marchant Radcliffe than that he's a good salesman.

What kind of guy is he, other than one who drinks?

I think back on what Lizzy and Hunter have been murmuring about him since that day at the hospital. Hunter thinks he's doing drugs, and Lizzy thinks he has anxiety or something. Apparently, since he left the hospital that day, no one's really seen him. He's not answering calls from anyone but Rachelle, the woman who helps him run the ranch, and he won't answer the door to his private cottage when Hunter knocks.

Lizzy says he's drowning in gambling debt because he can't stay away from blackjack. So he's a gambler *and* a drinker. Isn't that lovely?

I wonder what made Adam a drinker. Was it anxiety? I think that was a big part of it.

My thoughts are wandering to what my parents think about the news that Adam and I split, when I step out from beneath a copse of oak trees and I see the shrubbery maze, twisting like a square worm in the darkness. A few more steps, and I can see the shrubs are tall—easily taller than six feet—and in the warm breeze, their little leaves dance.

It would be stupid to go into a maze as it's getting dark. I'd probably get lost. And yet, I step in. The situation resembles my life right now so much, I almost hope I will get lost, just so I can have to work my way back out.

CHAPTER EIGHT

Suri

BY THE TIME I get back into our suite, I've decided that I'm leaving tomorrow. I'm not helping Cross, I'm not spending any time with Lizzy, and I'm startling at every turn, worried about whether an encounter with Marchant Radcliffe would result in me slapping him or jumping his bones.

I'm tucking clothes into my suitcase, about to put in a call for the plane to get me in the morning, when the door opens and Lizzy sticks her head inside.

"Suri?" Her eyes double in size. "What are you doing?"

"Liz, I'm sorry, but I just can't—"

"Suri—Suri, no." She steps in, shaking her head vehemently. "No. You can't go now. I need you here!"

Her proclamation irritates me. "That's ridiculous. You just spent the night with your gajillion hooker friends."

It's mean, okay? I know it's mean. But it's not *that* mean. So when Lizzy sits down on the bed, drops her head into her hands, and starts to sob, I'm shocked. I step over and throw an arm around her.

"Lizzy—hey, I'm sorry. I didn't mean to be so harsh, it's just, I saw Marchant Radcliffe and—"

"I'M PREGNANT!"

"…What?"

"I'M PREGNANT! No one knows! And earlier today, Hunter said children are…a blight!"

So that's what she's been so weird about. "Oh, Lizzy. Oh man. This is big news! But it'll be fine." I rub her back as she sobs. "You'll change his mind. He loves you and you're getting married."

"No we're not! We can't! I'll be too fat to—" she hiccups— "I'll be too fat to wear a dress!"

I pull her into my arms and hold her while she cries about stretch marks and pushing out a "ten pound vagina bomb" and try not to think about Marchant Radcliffe.

It's going to be a long night.

Marchant

I'M IN THE kitchen, about to pop an Ativan, when I hear a knock on the back door. I know it's Hawkins. I can *feel* it. And this time, I can shoot him, because he's trespassing.

I run downstairs and punch the glass out of my gun cabinet, grab a .38 and load it quickly. By the time I get to the kitchen, I've stuck the gun inside the back of my jeans, because I've managed to convince myself it's only Hunter. Or Rachelle. Or someone else coming to check on me.

But when I open the back door, I find myself staring at Hawkins—the little fuck.

He hits me in the face. Then two thugs grab me by the shoulders and haul me up against the stone wall of my house. I manage to reach my arm behind myself and dig my hand into the waist of my jeans. I work my sweaty fingers around the gun, and when I pull it free I point it toward Hawkins' legs. I am stunned by the boom as the bullet hits him in the foot. Blood sprays like a fucking geyser.

He howls, and the goons rush to his aid. I dart back inside my kitchen, slamming the door behind me just in time for the bullet that punches through it to miss me.

I look out the square window, and I see one of the goons pointing a pistol at me. I'm slightly surprised to find that I'm not worried. Then I see Hawkins holding up his hand to them—a silent 'stand down.' He grimaces as Goon One helps him stand, and I see that my wild shot probably just grazed him. Pity.

Hawkins hobbles to the door and presses his face against the glass, and his panted breaths makes clouds of fog. "You'll pay for this Radcliffe. I've given you more breaks…than I'd give my own damn cousin."

And I realize for the first time that it's not Monday. I don't know what day it is, but I know I missed the deadline to pay Hawkins. I even had the money moved—but I lost track of time.

Fuck!

Hawkins spits on my door, and then he and his crew turn to go. I realize, belatedly, that they're wearing dark clothes— hoods, even, unless my eyes are playing tricks on me.

It takes me a few minutes panting, chugging vodka from a bottle in my freezer, to calm down, and when I do, I realize I should call security. But as soon as I wrap my hand around my phone, someone bangs on my door. I mean really goes at it.

Shit. So the little bastard came back for another round. I chug some more Gray Goose and palm my gun. Then I pull the door open, stunned to see it's Juniper, wearing nothing but thigh-highs, a thong, and a lacy dark blue bra.

Her eyes are wide, her hair a mess. She waves her arms and screams, "MARCHANT! COME NOW! THERE'S A FIRE!"

CHAPTER NINE

Marchant

I DON'T NEED shoes or a shirt. I don't need anything but my gun. I clutch the .38 as I dash behind Juniper, cutting through the grass beside my cottage and following her willowy form toward the pond. I can smell the smoke already. We come around a few oak trees and I see the flames. They're bright—so bright they almost blind me. It's surreal.

I feel nothing but the burning of my muscles as I run toward the main house—nothing but that and the determination to get everyone out.

By the time I get within ball-throwing distance, the fire has engulfed most of the back left side of the building, and people are pouring out two sets of rear doors toward the right, even though our fire plan directs them to the front. I don't see Rachelle, and I feel a sick jolt of fear for her.

Where is Hunter?

Where is Suri Dalton?

Where is Hawkins?

My throat knots up as I realize this fire is his doing. *My* doing. If someone dies, it will be my fault.

I lean down in the bushes to be sick, then push through a frenzied group of escorts, clients, and staff, and run through one of the flame-framed doorways.

Heat engulfs me. My first breath burns my lungs, makes me cough on the exhale, makes my eyes tear.

Shit is falling from the walls and ceilings. Shit that's burning. The damn black smoke clouds the place so thickly I can hardly see. As I move past the bar into the great hall, where the stairs are, I catch something hard and heavy on my shoulder. It erupts in searing pain that burns itself out as I dash around bookshelves, past couches, screaming, "IS ANYBODY IN HERE?"

Fuck, it's hot. My bare chest and back feel like they're burning. I turn a circle in front of the elevator, struggling to get my bearings.

The ranch can't be on fire. It can't *be burning.*

I'm on the move again a second later. I find one of the chef's assistants covering her face with a towel in a downstairs hall and shove her out an emergency exit at the end of it. I find one of the newer girls—Bree—in a first-floor room, sobbing and screaming into her phone. I break the glass out of a window and send her out, shoving her a little as she crawls over the windowsill, into the grass, which is burning in some spots.

I'm coughing badly now. Every breath is more difficult to pull than the last. I'm dizzy—yeah. I realize that. I just don't care.

Getting upstairs is surprisingly easy. There's a hidden, staff stairwell near the exit door at the end of this first-floor hall that doesn't seem to be burning yet, and that's the route I take.

I catch a string of violent-sounding Spanish—one of the clients, I guess—behind me. I whirl, but no one is there. I take the rest of the stairs two at a time. As I reach the door at the top of the two-floor stairwell, I think I hear Hawkins' laughter. But I can't be sure. I'm probably hallucinating.

I shudder through a coughing fit before I stick my head into the second-floor hallway and call, "Is anybody there?"

I call out several times before someone screams,

"MARCHANT!"

I whirl, and there's Rachelle, stomping toward me. Her blonde hair is sweat-plastered to her head; her eyes are wild. She grabs my arm—"Are you fucking crazy?"—and hauls me back down the stairs.

The place is going fast. I can't believe it. The hall where the staff stairwell is, the one that leads to the great hall, is lined with fire along the baseboards. Fire writhes in patches on the ceiling. Beyond it, where the hallway meets the great room, I can't see anything but light. I think I hear screaming from that direction, but Rachelle starts to choke and cough, and I know I need to get her outside. I tug her out the nearest exit, throw her over my shoulder, and rush around the inferno, cutting through the grass to get her to the front of the building.

I sling her down by a bush that's not too close to the blaze and grab her face so I can see her eyes. They're red, just like her cheeks and forehead. "You okay? You breathing okay?"

She nods, and tugs on my arm until I help her stubborn ass up, and together we go through the crowd, checking on people, trying to account for others, and asking if anyone saw where the fire started. For some fucked up reason all I can think about is Suri Dalton, and I don't see her anywhere.

I see Libby DeVille—soot-smeared and crying—and I grab her arm. "Where is your friend?"

"Huh?"

"Where is Suri Dalton?"

Libby turns a circle, mouth agape. "Where *is* she? She was just here like one second ago!"

"I'll go find her," Hunter says.

"Oh my God, where's Cross?" Libby's eyes are huge. "I thought I saw him earlier, but—"

"I'll find them." I run around the house, dodging patches of fire on the lawn, focused on finding Carlson and Suri Dalton. I remember a foggy scene from the hospital hallway: me, dickishly asking if she had a thing for Carlson, but I push that aside as I round the house on the pool side. It's covered tonight, and debris is raining down on the smooth cement. I want to push it back, because a pool is good in a fire, right? I don't have time to waste, but still, I stop beside it. I'm dizzy as fuck and shaking with adrenaline and crazy, but I want to push the cement cover back. It's not a huge pool, but it might do something.

I kneel down and push the leaves of a withered fern aside, finding the button that controls the cement pool cover, and sit there coughing and cursing as burning shit bounces off my back.

There's something I'm supposed to do, but I can't remember it anymore.

As I wrack my mind, one of the last remaining first-floor doors flies open, and several men run out. They toss a cursory glance my way but keep moving toward the garden. It looks like they're—what the fuck? Are they packing AK-47s?

No way.

What the fuck?

I'm on my feet, ready to follow them, when someone grabs me by the waist. I whirl around, howling from the pain of grabbing hands on my sore skin—and find myself facing Suri Dalton. Her face is soot-smeared and red, her hazel eyes huge.

Relief washes through me. I grab her by the arms just to make sure she's real.

"Marchant, look," she cries, wriggling out of my grasp and whirling toward the house. She starts to cry, and without understanding what the fuck she's rambling about, I shove her forward. "Go around to the front! Give this place a wide berth; shit is falling. Find Rachelle and Hunter. Tell Hunter I just saw a bunch of cartel thugs—"

"They're here for Missy!" Suri grabs me by the elbow and tugs me toward the fire. "Look *up*, Marchant! What do we do?!"

"There's nothing we can do—" I say, looking into her eyes— "short of turning on the— I should turn on the emergency sprinkler system! Follow—"

"CROSS!" she screams, pointing, and I look up this time. "THAT'S CROSS UP THERE, MARCHANT!"

I follow her finger to find Carlson in one of the smoke-fogged, upstairs windows. I squint a little, and it looks like he's carrying someone on his shoulders.

I turn to Suri, planning to tell her that I'm going back in-side—but suddenly the cartel thugs are rushing past us, a whole fucking bunch of them dressed in fatigues, barking in Spanish, and pointing machine guns at the window over the pool, where Carlson stands.

Suri screams, and one of the Mexican fuckers looks her way, and I know that face: Jesus Cientos—a notorious drug lord who, I'm told, bought Missy King. Motherfucker's come to take her back, and he burned down my ranch to do it!

My aim is steady. I fire twice, and he goes down. The men around him jump on my ass—or try to. I shove Suri into the trees, then lead them around, toward the side of the house. Bullets whiz past me. I shoot back: BAM BLAM BAM click click— fuck! This fucking gun only holds five rounds!

Another of them topples into a bunch of shriveled ferns. I hear the first wail of the sirens, and the rest scatter. Seconds lat-er, there's an explosion of glass above me, and I look up to see a bulky shadow fall toward the pool.

Then there's water spraying everywhere, a fire truck rolling through the grass, men and women in uniforms hauling hoses and ladders. I'm walking backward, looking up at the main house. It's almost gone. It's already gone. Where is Suri Dalton?

I cup my hands around my mouth. "Suri? Suri!"

I shout her name for the longest time, dragging air into my stinging lungs, watching the place go down in pieces while it's sprayed with hoses. But they're too late. Way too late.

The air is black, the world is orange and red. It's hell and I *feel* like hell. And suddenly a police car is here, pulled up beside the pool. I stare at its lights, and for a second they are lights on the top of a car outside a mortuary in New Orleans. I'm going to jail for assaulting a doctor, and I don't fucking care. As quickly as the memory comes, it goes.

Where is Suri Dalton?

I stumble forward a few steps—so close the heat stings me—and find myself staring into the eyes of a middle-aged police officer with a thin mustache.

"Marchant Radcliffe?"

I nod.

"I'm Officer Dirk Eilhert with the county police. I'm not sure where you're headed off to, but I'm gonna ask that you stay put. We need you to—"

"No!" I shake my head. "I need to make sure everyone's okay."

"We've been working with the EMTs and we're told no one is trapped inside."

"Are you sure? When did they tell you that?"

"Just now."

"Who'd they get that info from?"

"Manager. I believe the name was Rachel."

Rachelle. My shoulders loosen. "Good."

"Do you have any idea how the fire—"

"Hell yeah I do." I point to the body by a burning chunk of house. "Jesus Cientos did this. Mexican drug lord motherfucker."

"I know who he is, sir. How did he go down?"

I look from the body to the cop. "I shot him."

His eyes widen even more, and I wonder if I should be saying these things. He writes something on his clip board, and says, "I need you to wait until we can take you down to the station for your statement—"

"No." I shake my head. "I'm not leaving. I'll do it here."

It takes forever for the right person to arrive, and I forget what I tell him the moment the words leave my mouth, but they work, because he leaves me with his card.

I talk to Rachelle, to Hunter and to Libby. I help people into their cars and thank the firefighters as they start coming down from their ladders. I don't see Suri Dalton.

Smoke is pouring off the building. It's black. Nothing but a stone shell.

I wander around it a few times, aware that other people are here, but not sure who they are or what they're doing. It's so dark. It doesn't matter.

Someone comes and wants to talk about insurance, but I tell him to come back later. "It was arson," I say. "Just ask the cops."

I drift toward the pool and stand there, looking in the direction of the gardens, of my cottage, where my guns are. I pull a .38 out of my pocket, suddenly surprised that I have it.

I don't want that thing. I don't like guns. I throw it into some bushes, beside a fountain, and walk toward the pool.

My skin hurts. I'm hot. I need to get in the water.

I walk in with my eyes on the blackened shell before me. I'm choking on the smoke, but I don't care. I'm not leaving.

The water's cold—surprisingly so—and for a second my whole body freezes up. I know I should probably get out—I'm gonna send myself into some kind of shock, going from hot to cold like this—but the sensation is mind-numbing. I take a few more steps into the water, deep enough now so it laps at my chin.

I look up at the sky, an army of stars blotted by writhing smoke. An army of stars, looking down on the ruin all around me. I sink in to my nose, and as the water seeps into my ears, I remember something I heard a long time ago. Something I read somewhere I can't even begin to remember, but for this sentence: "For death is no more than a turning of us over from time to eternity."

I look up at the stars again. Then I open my mouth and inhale water.

Suri

THE COPS ARE still here, so I'm not alone. There are a few firefighters, too, asking me to stay away from the building as I walk around it, looking in the charred grass for my grandmother's emerald ring. I know I won't find it, but I have to look.

As I search the dark grass with a flashlight app on my phone, I remember how blistered Meredith's skin looked when they loaded her into the ambulance, and how lost Cross looked beside her. That was the first moment I've felt at peace about Adam's and my breakup. At peace about Cross and his choices, and about what happened between the two of us. Before the ambulance doors shut, Cross hugged me, and it felt like we were friends again. After the ambulance doors shut, I thought about the look on Cross's face—one of total devastation—and I knew Adam wouldn't have looked that way about me. He would have been upset and unhappy, sure, but never devastated. Honestly, I can't say I would have been devastated if that had been Adam in the ambulance.

I glance up at what remains of the building. Made to look like an English manor house, the "main house" was made of stone and wood. It's situated between two smaller replicas; one of which got burned some, the other of which did not. The main house, of course, is all but gone.

I wonder how hot the fire must have been to crumple the stone. The building is still pouring smoke, emitting enough heat to make me sweat from thirty feet away. In some places, you can see down to the charred twigs of the house's foundation. In one spot, I can see what's left of a large bed-frame.

It's hard to believe that a few hours ago this place was fully operational and now it's just…decimated. Gone, the beauty of the rugs and bookshelves. Gone, my luggage and clothes. Gone, the open bar, the plush beds, soft rugs.

Less than three hours ago, I was consoling Lizzy about her pregnancy. How did that night turn into *this*? How could anyone be so filled with hate and evil that they chase a victimized woman into another country and try to kill her?

It makes me feel ill.

I look up when I see the darting blue-green light coming from the pool. A light breeze ripples the water's surface, casting shadows through the glowing water. It's so pretty, compared to the devastation around it, that for a second I just stare. And that's when I notice: *There's something big and dark at the bottom.*

I walk slowly forward, because the firefighters have said to be cautious, and the pool is right behind the charred remains of the house. My eyes are trained on the object at the bottom of the water—something about it tugs at my attention, but I have no idea what it is. A chunk of the roof? A piece of the window Cross and Merri jumped out of?

I step onto the pool's cement deck, and all the air goes out of my lungs.

Holy shit, that's a *person!*

I hesitate for a moment—long enough to ask myself if this person might still be alive—before realizing I'm wasting precious time. I kick my shoes off and dive into the deep end of the heart-shaped pool.

The water is breathtakingly cold. I open my eyes and kick toward the bottom, stretching my arms to reach for this person.

It's dark at the bottom of the pool, so it isn't until I've grabbed the person's large shoulders that I see the outline of his face.

NO FREAKING WAY.

It's him.

It's Marchant Radcliffe, I think.

I know.

The shock of it is almost enough to send me racing for the surface. But I can see him laughing at my panic. I thread my arms under his, kick off the bottom of the pool, and scissor my legs as hard and fast as I ever have.

Don't be dead.

Please, you freaking asshole, don't be dead.

Oh God, what if he's dead?

I can barely get my face above the water; he's so heavy. When I do, I take a deep breath and begin to sob.

"Marchant... Oh, Marchant. Shit. Oh shit." I'm babbling as I kick, reaching for the pool's side. I grab onto a metal ladder and I let myself sink a little, swimming beneath him to turn him over, face up. His hair is in his eyes and his face is limp and life-less as I scream, "HELP! HELP, HELP! HELP ME, PLEASE!"

I can't get him out of the pool, so I wrap my legs around the ladder and clutch his torso. His face is so pale. Is he breathing? I can't see his chest move. I grab his chin. Isn't that part of CPR? It is. It definitely is. Except there's water in his lungs! Surely there's water in his lungs and how do you do CPR if there's water in the lungs?!

"HELP ME! HELP!"

Why won't anybody come?

I try to tilt his head back but he starts to sink. Shit! I don't have a good enough grip on him. I hear footsteps and clutch him closer to me, kicking hard to keep my head above water, craning my head so I can see, over my shoulder, two figures moving fast with clomping footsteps.

"HELP ME! PLEASE!"

With difficulty, I turn a little more and see two EMTs—a man and a woman—reach for us.

"Oh my God! Oh my God! I think he might have drowned!"

Faster than I can get the words out, they haul him up out of the water and dump him face down on the deck. I scramble up the ladder. I stand there dripping, shaking violently, while one of them pounds on his back and the other one messes with his head.

Please let him live. Please God, let him live.

They roll him onto his side. While the man holds his head, the woman does something to his mouth. They push him onto his back. One of them shouts something, and then the woman begins CPR.

"Marchant, please! You've got to breathe!" I'm sobbing, now on my knees. I reach out, because I feel like I should touch him, but one of the EMTs knocks my hand away.

The next second, Marchant's body heaves, the woman rolls him on his side, and I can see his back heave as he gets sick.

The paramedics hold his shoulders, and the night is filled with retching sounds and the splash of water on cement. I scoot away to give them space, but I can't take my eyes off him. It's impossible to reconcile: this image with the one from the bathroom at the Wynn. The charming rogue who held my hand, and later, at the hospital, the drunken asshole. His shoulders are shaking now. He's groaning and gasping, almost sobbing. I can't see him from the front, but suddenly I wish I could. I wish I was holding him.

I take a few steps closer, and the woman barks, "Stay back!"

I take a step back, then turn because I hear an ambulance cutting through the grass. It parks close and two people jump out, one with oxygen and the other with a neck brace and a board.

They all converge over Marchant as he's rolled onto his back. They're speaking quickly, but I hear, "found him in the pool..."

"...administered CPR..."

"...pulse is weak..."

All too soon, they're lifting him onto a stretcher and strapping down his legs.

He makes a terrible groaning noise and tries to pull the oxygen mask off his face, and they strap down his arms and someone holds the oxygen on. He starts shaking, violent shaking, and they turn his head sideways so he can be sick again.

More water.

When he's finished, he's moaning and gripping the sides of his stretcher.

They take off toward the ambulance, and I dash after them. It's not my place. I know that, but I can't help myself. I put my hand on the door of the ambulance as they set him down inside. When one of them gives me an inquiring look, I blurt, "I feel like I should come with him."

"Well, come on."

The doors slam shut behind me, and I scramble to a little seat by his head.

The ambulance jolts into motion, and all I can think is *this was a mistake*. I don't belong here. The EMTs are pulling his jeans down and I can see his hips, and they're beautiful—underwear model hips—but I have no right to them. He keeps opening and closing his mouth under the mask, and his eyes peek open and drift shut, and his hands still clench the stretcher.

I can't do anything but sit here while he shivers and clenches his jaw and opens and closes his mouth like a fish. He takes a few deep, raspy-sounding breaths, and the EMTs fly into motion again.

I pick a spot on his side to stare at, but I don't like the frenzied way his chest is moving, so I train my attention on his arm. It's well-shaped, well-muscled, like he works out a lot. I take a deep breath and wonder if I should take his hand or something. I climbed into the ambulance. Shouldn't I at least, I don't know, put my hand on his arm?

Maybe I shouldn't.

Maybe he wouldn't even want that.

I don't know what he would want.

I don't think he's awake, or aware at all, but when they start to jab a needle into the crook of his arm, his eyes flip open. He blinks twice in quick succession, taking in his surroundings, and then he fixes his eyes on the woman sticking him.

"STOP!" he roars. "NO NEEDLES!"

My heart thunders as he strains against the restraints. Then he pops through the restraints, jetting up into a sitting up position, and looks dazedly around the inside of the ambulance. His eyes land on me and they widen. "Suri Dalton."

I nod, reaching for him. "It's okay," I murmur. "Just lie down. You'll be okay."

He shakes his head at me and turns back to the EMTs. "No more IVs," he says sternly, even though his voice is breathy and cracked. "I don't...do needles."

He gives me a brief look, one that's helpless, infuriated, and confused at once, and then he passes out.

CHAPTER TEN

Suri

WHEN WE ARRIVE at the ER, I rip a page out of Lizzy's book and tell the intake nurse that I'm Marchant's kin: his cousin, as I have no fake ID.

When I'm allowed into the sick bay, I find Marchant in a half-seated position, under a thick, gray blanket, shivering slightly, looking perturbed.

A pretty blonde nurse is telling him his burns need to be treated, but he shakes his head. "It doesn't hurt. I'm fine."

"You're his...cousin?" the nurse asks me.

I nod, and Marchant arches a skeptical eyebrow.

The nurse shifts her weight, now facing me. "Your cousin has burns on his back and his hands, and he's refusing treatment."

I step closer, tentatively taking one of his wrists. His hands are red and blistered. I wince. "That's got to hurt."

"I can't feel it," he says simply.

"Well it needs treatment anyway." I look from his petulant face to the nurse's concerned one. "Why don't you bandage it or do whatever you would do."

She blows her breath out. "To do that, we'll need to give him an injection of numbing medicine."

"Can you do it without that?"

She frowns. "It would be unethical. Excruciating."

"And there's no other option? Nothing you could, say, paint onto his skin or spray on?"

"Not really."

I look at Marchant's face. It's burned deep pink on the forehead and cheeks. His lips are cracked. His eyes are wild. "Are you sure you can't do needles?"

He nods once, looking as desperate as he did on Hunter's plane.

I turn back to the nurse. "There's got to be something else. Some kind of spray."

"Nothing that would be effective."

I'm shocked when he climbs out of the bed. He's still wet, he's pale as death, and he's wearing only slacks. His hair drips as he turns to look at me.

"Thanks for your help," he says. "But you shouldn't have."

And then he's out the door.

Marchant

I HEAR SURI Dalton scrambling behind me as I stride through the hospital parking lot. She's calling my name, I think. I can hardly hear her over the rush of blood inside my head.

I pick up the pace, hoping she'll get the point and turn around. Instead, I hear the patter of her bare feet on the asphalt, and her tiny hand closes around my bicep. "Do you have your wallet?" she asks as I come to a halt. "Marchant, can you even call a cab?"

Careful not to look her in the eye, I point to a hotel across the street. "No cab needed."

"Do you have any money for a room?"

I inhale deeply. I don't, of course, but at the moment I don't care. Maybe I'll just sleep outside.

"Let me come with you. Let me at least get you a room, and then I'll leave if you want."

"Fine."

I stride ahead of her, because I can't stand to look her in the face. I'm so fucking embarrassed. That she's here right now, seeing me like this.

There's no telling what I might say or do right now. I think I'm nearing the end of this shit—I think I've begun to feel the icy fingers of depression work their way into my chest—but I can't say for sure. I haven't been this fucked up since college.

I weave between rows of parked cars, and I hear her on my heels. I'm having trouble breathing—my lungs still feel wet, and they're burned to boot—so I slow down, and I feel her hand on my back.

Humiliation and shame twist through me. "You don't have to do this." I turn around to scowl at her. "I don't need your help."

"Okay." She says it slowly, like she's speaking to a petulant child. "You can pay me back if you like."

Payback reminds me of Hawkins, which sends a cold wash of guilt over me. Then I remember abruptly that Cientos started the fire—he came for Missy King—and I shot him. Didn't I? I can hardly remember.

"Where's Hunter?" I ask, rubbing my forehead. It's just occurred to me that there were other people in the fire. Almost everyone I know and care about. I turn around to face Dalton. "Are he and Libby okay?"

She nods. "They're at another hospital with Cross and Meredith."

"Meredith?"

"She…used to go by Missy."

I nod slowly. I remember that now. Cars whoosh past us on the road between the hospital and the hotel across the street. "What happened to them?"

"Missy's really bad, they said. I mean, Meredith."

"Do you know if anyone else was hurt?"

She shakes her head. "Everyone got out, though."

I feel a swell of guilt about the whole thing, and especially for Missy. I told her she'd be safe with me. I didn't keep my promise. I wonder if Cientos found her before Cross Carlson did.

"I remember…" I swallow hard, looking down at Suri Dalton's beautiful bare feet. "I remember the window."

Suri nods. "Cross and Merri jumped out the window, into the pool. Marchant…" she starts; her eyebrows pull together, all concerned, and I know where she's going. I know what she's asking. And I don't intend to tell her one damn thing.

I turn around and start across the busy street. I don't give a fuck that I'm not wearing shoes or a shirt. I don't care that there's no crosswalk either. As I dash through traffic, I feel confident I'll be alone when I get to the hotel parking lot.

I clear the curb, and a patch of grass pokes my bare feet. I glance at Dalton, who is one step behind me. I fix her with a 'fuck off' look and try to set things right. "Could you go? I'd like to be alone."

The breeze blows a strand of hair across her rosy cheeks, and I watch her mouth as she bites down on her lower lip. "I'm not going to do that."

"Why not?"

"Because you almost died tonight, for one."

I sneer. "What's two?"

She looks me over, head to toe. Her lips pinch. "Because you're a raging mess. I think you need me."

"You fucking wish."

She's shivering violently now, wrapping her arms over her chest, where I can see hard nipples through her shirt. Her pretty face is hard; pissed off. Score one for me. "No I don't, you arrogant ass. I wish I was at home, in my warm bed. But I'm here, with you, because I found you at the bottom of a fucking *pool*! What's wrong with you?"

The wind carries her voice across the hotel parking lot, where it dies amidst a line of neatly parked cars and SUVs.

I take a step closer to her, hoping to evoke emotion in myself. But when I look into her hazel eyes, I feel nothing.

"Go the fuck away," I tell her. I inject a heavy dose of disdain into my voice and add a dismissive wave I hope will piss her off enough to make her disappear.

I can feel the darkness start to gather in me, collecting just below my throat like a weight on my breastbone. I need her to go before things with me get bad again.

She shakes her head. "I'm not leaving."

"I don't need a fucking friend."

But those big eyes are irrationally kind. *Did you do it on purpose?* That's what she's wondering, but she would never put it into words. Funny, because I almost want her to. I dare her with my eyes, and her gaze drops down to our feet. When she looks back up, her face is sad.

I stuff my hands in my jeans pockets, enjoying the way the denim burns my singed skin as I try it one more time. "I said *go the fuck away*."

She tosses her damp hair over her shoulders and gives me a tired sigh. "After I get your room," she says. "If that's what you really want."

We walk in silence past the curbside drop-off and through the automatic doors. She goes to the desk while I pace around by the coffee machines. I can hear her talking in hushed tones to the clerk, and I wonder what the fuck she's saying. Finally, she turns around, armed with a little paper packet of room cards.

She hands them to me, but she doesn't leave. When I head to the elevators, she follows me. I don't look at her. Not when she pushes the "2" button, and not when she gets off the elevator before I do. I don't look at her as I clench and unclench my hands because I'm feeling so damn edgy.

She gets a card into the door before I can, and pushes it open. As she steps away, those pretty hazel eyes peek up at me. "You sure you want me to go?"

I don't know what I want. I don't know anything—except I fucking hate myself.

So I do the worst thing I can do. I grab her shoulders and kiss her.

CHAPTER ELEVEN

Suri

THIS IS ENTIRELY different than the time at the Wynn.

He's forceful this time—from the moment he grabs my shoulders and spins me around so he can take my mouth. There's this millisecond when his lips first touch mine where I have a choice. Where I can pull away if I want. But I don't.

Because I pulled him up from the bottom of a pool but I'm not sure I saved his life. Because he is both cruel and broken, and despite both, my body screams for his.

When his lips touch mine, I can barely keep my knees from giving way.

Marchant sweeps the door open and wraps an arm around me, dragging me toward the king-sized bed. He turns me around and urges me down onto my back, with my legs hanging off the side of the mattress. He parts my knees and stands between them, leaning down over me so he can kiss my throat, my chin, my cheeks, and finally—when I can't stand it anymore—my mouth.

His lips close over mine with a harsh groan, and I sink my hands into his wild hair and pull him down on me. His body is warm and hard. I run my fingers from his biceps down his taut sides, and they leave trails of goosebumps. He's hard in seconds, pressing himself urgently against me.

I can feel his abs jerk as he breathes between our kisses: ragged breaths that do nothing to slow the fury of his mouth on mine.

His taste is a drug—hot and sweet and just a little salty.

With all thought stalled by the rhythm of our mouths and hands, I notice everything about the way he moves and feels. How when he breathes, his ribcage presses into mine so hard it hurts. Each and every kiss brings him down on me a little heavier. There's something predatory about the way he grabs my shoulder, yanks my hair, nips at my neck, crawls up on the bed and tosses me back a few feet. He climbs up on top of me, and I'm reminded of a lion.

Rough becomes forceful, almost painful. My mouth feels bruised, yet when he wrenches his away to grab a breath, my hand around his neck pulls him back down for more. Another hit. A feeding frenzy.

We're both slick with sweat, and salty. Licking, nipping, stroking, pinching. His hands slide down my hips and underneath my ass. He lifts me up and pushes his hips down. The room spins. I need him inside of me.

And then his hands are gone. His mouth is wrenched off mine. He pants above me, looking into my eyes with his wild brown ones.

"Why are you here?"

I remember the sensation of dragging him up from the bottom of the pool. Trying to kick enough for both of us. How heavy he was; how still. Does it count as saving if he didn't want it? The question sits inside my mouth, because I don't know how to ask it.

I swallow instead and whisper through my sore lips, "Because...I want to feel something."

His kisses are gentler when he eases back down on me. He lifts my shirt up, then slides one hand down my hip and peels back my yoga pants. As his hand finds me where I'm wet, his eyes widen.

"You're beautiful, woman. Fucking beautiful."

He crawls down and his mouth joins his hand, and I come quickly. It's like the sky being torn in two. He does it again, and again, until I'm quivering and exhausted. Then he lies beside me and kisses my neck.

I palm him through his slacks and find him hard as stone. I fumble with the button of his pants, finally pull them down, then sit up to urge him down onto his back. I stare for a moment at his naked abs and hips and thighs. There's something beautiful about his shape.

I long to know what the tattoo means, but I don't dare ask. I don't even touch it.

Instead, I stroke his hard length up and down, loving the way his thighs tense and his ass tightens and he lifts himself up off the bed to meet my hand. His hands grip my biceps. His eyes squeeze shut. I'm cradling his balls and stroking him a little faster when I decide I'd like to have him in my mouth.

I'm leaning over to do just that when he makes a strangled sound deep in his throat and spurts into my hands.

"Oh Christ," he murmurs. He turns over on his side and raises an arm to cover his face.

I watch the smooth slab of his side as his lungs expand and then constrict. I watch as he gets up, never looking at me, and half-stumbles into the bathroom, returning a minute later with grave eyes, wearing nothing but his boxer-briefs and a look that jabs me right below the ribs.

He shoves me back down on the bed and climbs over me, nipping at my neck. Kissing me gently near my shoulder. His breath on my skin is soft and warm; his hands threading through my hands feel cool. His voice sounds soft and tired when he says, "You should go now, Beauty."

I lift my forehead so it's pressed against his. "I don't want to."

I stroke my fingers down his back and feel the goosebumps. I tickle my hand down to the elastic of his boxer-briefs and sneak a finger inside them, where I shock both of us by teasing his crack. He draws a shuddering breath and I can feel his body tense.

"If you don't go now...you might not like the outcome," he says against my throat. As if to accentuate the point, he lifts his head. His eyes are wide. "I mean it."

I smile a little, caressing the hair that curves around his ear. "You called me Beauty a second ago. Does that make you Beast?"

His mouth tightens. "It's not a joke." He lifts off me and tugs me by my wrist. "Go, before I throw you down face first and fuck you like I want to."

I'm feeling high in this moment. Lust-drunk and powerful. Like I can keep him on this bed as long as I want to, and turn that frown upside down.

So I say, "Do it."

He grabs me by my hips and spins me, positioning me on hands and knees so my ass is in the air. He yanks my pants all the way off and slams his finger into me, stroking ruthlessly as his mouth covers my asshole.

I open my mouth to protest, but it's only a breath before I realize it feels good. So good I'm falling forward with my belly pressed against the mattress. My legs can barely keep me up, and then he's clutching my ass cheek, pumping my cunt, licking me with broad strokes of his tongue, and I'm gasping like I might pass out.

I might pass out.

He gets me close—so close—before he pulls his fingers out and moves his hot mouth off me. I draw my quivering knees in, and he slides his body underneath me so I'm on top. With a dark grin, he reaches down to find my pussy with his fingers again. It's tighter now, and I'm curled over, desperate. "Don't stop..."

I stroke my finger down his chest and lean down so my other hand caresses his head. His eyes harden. "Are you on birth control?"

I open my mouth to say it isn't necessary, but he cuts me off. "Are you on birth control?"

I nod—to simplify things.

"You take it regularly?"

"Yes," I lie. "But I also have a condom if you want it."

He nods and I reach past him for my clutch, the only thing in reach when the fire started. I've got some fire-engine red, cherry-flavored condoms in it from that night with Adam at the gala.

I turn back around to find him sitting on his knees. His dick juts out ridiculously, and I'm surprised to find myself gasping with eagerness to feel it inside me. His hands, I've noticed, look chapped and painful, so I scoot closer and roll the latex over his plump head.

He closes his eyes as I fit it on him. He's bigger than Adam, so it's snug. Below his thickness, his balls look taut and heavy.

I'm trembling as he leans closer. The tip of him brushes my thigh as he takes off my front-clasp bra and leans down to kiss my breasts. I shove him away and move my mouth as fast as I can to his dick. I caress those swollen balls as I stroke a shaft. He comes in half a minute, leaning over me and pulling on my hair.

"Oh God," he groans.

I smile as he stretches out on his back, staring without blinking at the ceiling.

"Can I?" I gesture to his cock, which is somehow still hard and ready. He nods a little. I tug the condom off and find a garbage can. When I return, already wondering if he wants more, I find him on his side, facing the air conditioning unit, with his broad, heat-chapped back to me. His breathing is shallow and fast.

I sit down behind him, feeling almost ill with concern. "Are you okay?"

"Don't ask me that."

"Why not?"

"Because this isn't that. It's just a fuck."

"Okay," I murmur.

"Is it?" His voice is low. Almost challenging.

"I knew what I was getting into when I came in here with you. I know you're a drinker and a fighter and—"

"And what?" He turns around to face me, and I swear I think his eyelashes are wet. His face looks hard and angry.

"You're not always nice."

"No—I'm not."

He grabs my wrists and pushes me down on my back, raising my arms above my head and pressing them down into the mattress.

His face twists. "You think you know me?" His eyes are hard—so hard and empty, I find my lips trembling before I whisper, "No."

"You made a mistake." His mouth tightens, and he squeezes my wrists harder. Then, for half a second, his eyes soften. He murmurs, "Do you want to go?"

I swallow hard and shake my head.

"If you stay, I'm going to fuck you." He releases one wrist and runs his fingertips feather lightly down my belly. "Do you want to be fucked, Suri Dalton?"

He spreads my legs and lowers his face over my throbbing cunt.

"Answer me," he murmurs, tracing a finger down my slit. I'm so wet, he glides between my lips with ease, pausing over my entrance to tease me with his thumb. I press my hips up, desperate to feel his fingers stretching inside of me.

"Answer me!"

"YES!" I half-sob.

He glides his fingertip over my clit, and I try to lift my hips to him. My legs are almost useless. I'm trembling so hard I can barely move.

"Wait here," he tells me. "Do not move."

He grabs another condom from my bag and quickly rolls it over himself.

Then he gathers both my arms in his big hand, holding them firmly over my head, and moves his hips so he's teasing me.

"Come on, Marchant... Please!"

He slams inside me—hard and fast, and I scream.

When he leaves me panting in the shower several hours later, I'm not sure if I feel broken or empowered. All I know for certain is I want more.

CHAPTER TWELVE

Marchant

"RIGHT THIS WAY, Mr. Radcliffe."

I follow the nurse down a long, white hall, and force my legs to stay steady as she slides an ID through a card reader beside a stainless steel door. It makes a soft clicking sound, and she pushes it open, revealing a small, white room dominated by a wide hospital bed and several large machines.

"We've spoken with your regular psychiatrist." She motions to the bed, and I climb onto it. I'm so exhausted I can hardly see straight, so it's an effort to keep the damn gown shut. "She said you've experienced a lengthy manic phase that's likely winding down. Are you sure you want this?"

I shake my head. "I *need* this. I'm sure."

I think about the day I flushed my Lithium down the toilet. March 15. I think about March 15, 2007, and I'm sure.

She nods. "Okay. Just try to relax. I'll be back soon."

I lie back on the bed and close my eyes. I see a golden casket. I feel the cool leather of the squad car seat behind my back. My memory thrusts me back in time, several hours earlier, that day, and I remember breaking the arms of another man in a white coat.

"I'm gonna fucking kill you, you motherfucking murderer!"

117

I remember, hours before that, the phone call from Marissa. Telling me what had happened. Telling me what she'd done. Sobbing.

"You told me to! You told me to do it Marchant!"

I squeeze my eyes more tightly shut, and I try to remember the words I said that changed the course of both our lives. But I never can. Because I was manic. Because I was possessed.

I'm tired of being manic.

I'm tired of being me.

I'm tired.

When the nurse returns, she's got a couple of other nurses, and two doctors, with her. The doctor in charge hands me the paperwork, and I skim over the risks and side-effects.

Memory loss. I pray for that. I pray for that as I sign consent and they begin to prep me.

"You'll do several treatments. We'll decide on an exact number based on how you respond to this first one."

I nod.

One of the nurses grabs my arm, and I have to struggle to keep breathing regularly.

"I'll make the injection fast, okay?"

I nod again. Then I shut my eyes, relax my arm. Force myself to look straight ahead, rather than into the nurse's face.

The needle sinks into my arm, and darkness claims me. The last thing I imagine before the curtain falls on everything is Suri Dalton.

"YOU SHOULD HAVE told me sooner."

I nod. I want to say, "I know," but I can't get my mouth to work. I guess this is how it is, getting back on my meds. I'm also taking something new they gave me at the hospital.

I lie down on my bed and stare at the ceiling. Somewhere

far away, I'm aware that Rachelle has walked into the kitchen. I'm alone in my room, for the first time since I ran from my garden house toward the fire.

I still kind of want to die, but it's not as bad anymore.

Probably because I just don't have the energy.

Sometime later, I hear Rachelle say something to me and I turn my head toward her. She's standing by my bed, holding a tray bearing a bowl of soup and a sleeve of Ritz crackers. I blink a few times at her. Make enough circuits fire to say, "Thank you."

I'm hoping she will go now, but she doesn't. She lies on the bed beside me and shares my pillow. I can smell her perfume: Stella. Her head nudges my shoulder, and I feel her eyes on me. "You okay, M? Really?"

I nod.

"I've got your pills, okay? Libby will be back in two days. She told me in the meantime, we can cut way back on Diazepam. You seem pretty out of it."

I nod. It's for the best that I'm sedated.

"I'm going to fourth it tonight, okay? You'll be left with just your Lithium. I think you'll be fine. There's nothing in this house that should bother you. I took care of it."

She means the knives and guns. And tempt me, not bother me. "I'm sorry, Rachelle." My voice sounds thick. Not like mine.

Good. I don't want to be me anymore.

"This isn't your fault, Marchant. None of it is. Maria has OCD, remember? I understand how these things work." Maria is Rachelle's partner.

I nod again.

"Do you remember what happened with Jesus Cientos?"

I shake my head. I know I shot him, but I don't really remember it.

"You did a lot of people a service."

I blink a few times. I don't have the energy to think of that.

"Good," I say. And then, "I want to start rebuilding."

Rachelle, who's lying on her side now with her head propped on her palm, is frowning at me. "You already found a contractor. Before you left the hospital. You offered to pay them double if they finished fast."

I nod. I don't remember, and I wish I hadn't promised *double* the money, but, "Good. I want the same floor plan. But I think I want to change up everything else."

"We need to hire someone for the aesthetics, obviously."

I stare up at my ceiling and say the name that's always on my lips these days. "Suri Dalton."

Rachelle hesitates only a second—I don't look at her, but I know she's giving me a look. "You want me to set up a consult?"

"No." I'm not going to ask her.

"Okay. Just keep me posted." Rachelle gets up. I think she says some other stuff, but it's hard to make myself listen. So much easier to just lie here.

Eventually she says, "Should I show myself out?"

"Sure."

She groans. "Come on now, March. Sit up and eat your soup." I sit up slowly, and under her watchful eye shove a spoonful into my mouth.

She waves her cell phone. "Call me if you need me."

I nod. "Thanks."

Sometime later, I blink down at my uneaten soup and swing off the bed. I should lock the door behind her.

I'm walking back to my bed when I get the text: *Hope the insurance money comes in soon.*

It's from an unknown number, but I know who it is. Hawkins.

Maybe the fire wasn't for Missy King after all.

Suri

WHEN CROSS, LIZZY, and I were in high school, we climbed a barbed wire fence around a few hundred acres of valley vineyard belonging to a former Hollywood stuntman named Bonnie McFarland. Word was, Bonnie had suffered one too many concussions and had gone a little crazy. We knew for sure that he had a pack of Dobermans. But Cross had made a bet with a guy in the grade above us about who could steal the flag Bonnie flew above his wine cellar first—so over the fence we went.

Lizzy had a trash bag full of meat and eggs to distract the Dobermans, and I had a can of mace, but the moment my feet hit the ground on the McFarland side of the fence, I heard the Dobermans snarl and I seriously thought I might stroke out.

That's how I feel right now, as I park my rented silver Jeep Grand Cherokee beside the charred ruins of what was the largest of the Love Inc. buildings.

I'm doing something risky—something that scares me. I'm here to look for Marchant Radcliffe. Because I want to have sex with him again. Scratch that. I want to fuck him again. Because that's what we did. We fucked. It was dirty. It was rough. And…I liked it. A lot.

But it's not just sex. Since he left me in the bathroom that night, I can't stop thinking about him. The person. I wonder, over and over, what happened to put him in the bottom of a pool. I wonder what the tattooed date means.

It's stupid. Yes. I know. Maybe he isn't worth my attention, but I'm intrigued, and for once, I'm single. Free. The risks are low. I'm not chained to him like I was Adam. If something goes wrong, there aren't any messy details to deal with: I just walk. If things went well…maybe I could find out who he really is.

So before I fly back home tomorrow, I decided to drive to the ranch and see if I run into him. If I do, I'm giving myself permission to do something crazy. Something stupid. I'm in charge. I can handle it. If I don't, I'll go back to L.A. feeling just a little freer.

My cover story is that I'm here to find my grandma's ring, but that's not true. I've already hired a team of experts to pick this place apart tomorrow.

I'll give a cursory look, but the truth is, I want to end up in Marchant's bed.

It's been six days since I last saw him. In the six days since, Lizzy told Hunter about the pregnancy, and he hauled her off to Napa, where he thinks she should rest. Cross has gone there, too, so he can re-open the motorcycle shop he shut down after his wreck. Merri's going to help him while she gets her life sorted out. They've hired a body guard to keep her safe, but she also has an FBI handler.

Just two days ago, I found out Adam is moving back to Napa…and in with Brina. It's weird, but I can't say I'm jealous. Adam and I were never meant to be together. Still, the thought of him with Brina is…unnerving. But I guess that's another reason to hook-up with Marchant: so I don't have to go back home quite yet.

It's five-thirty on a Thursday, but there's a big cement truck parked just in front of me, and I see a surprising number of workers milling around the beginnings of the new building. I don't know who else is here, or if anybody is.

According to Lizzy, Hunter hasn't been able to track Marchant down since the night of the fire. The most he could get out of Rachelle was that Marchant went on some sort of "vacation," but she wouldn't say when he would be back.

Hunter suspects he went to rehab. I've wondered for days

now if it's true. For some reason, I have a difficult time imagining Marchant in rehab. I guess I just can't see him taking orders from anyone. Then again, I have trouble imagining Marchant doing drugs—despite the many signs he likely does.

After a few minutes checking my hair and make-up in the visor mirror, I get out of the Jeep and face the ruins. It's really bad. Everything has been knocked to the ground, where it's a big pile of basically…trash, to the left of the pool. In front of the pool, poured over charred ground that looks as big as half a football field—or maybe even bigger—is a cement foundation. And over the cement, the plywood scaffolding of a new building. I hope it gets finished soon. Not because I'm a fan of what goes on here, but because no one deserves to lose their business.

I pull my rented metal detector out of the back of the Jeep, turn it on, and start around the cement truck. The workers wave at me, and I wave back. I hold my breath when I near the pool and walk quickly past it. I don't want to remember that part of my night with Marchant. I've metal-detected my way almost to the pond when I notice, in the low light of dusk, one of the girls waving at me from near the maze. I squint and see it's the nicest one, Loveless.

I wave back, and she jogs over, meeting me in the soft, shin-length grass surrounding the pond. "Hi. How's it going?" I ask her as we meet beside the sunset-streaked water.

"March gave us the week off, but I wanted to check on him before I left." She smiles. "And I hear we have you to thank for his continued existence. You're a hero."

I shake my head. "It was fortune, I think. I had lost my grandmother's ring, so I was hanging around trying to find it."

She nods at the long wand in my hands. "Still looking?"

"Yep. And I wanted to see your maze again. I do interior design, but I've got a client on the books in May who is interested in a formal garden. I figured I might walk through it another time."

"That thing makes me nervous."

"Nervous?"

She laughs. "Have you ever seen 'The Shining'?"

I nod. "I guess I see how it could be creepy." I look in that direction, seeing the cottages beyond the maze. "So is the brothel shut down? There's another one in town, right?"

Loveless nods. "A few of the girls are taking clients out of the cottages, but it's mostly shut down. We don't do business in town. It's a different place." A less exclusive one, from what I've heard. "I'm going to visit my dad for a few days, now that everything's more settled here." She glances at the cottages and bites her pretty, glossed lip. Then her eyes meet mine. "I'm sorry to be nosey, but do you know Marchant very well?"

I shake my head.

She shrugs. "He keeps to himself, but he's a good boss. I feel sorry for him, losing so much. He's worked hard to make this place what it is. You want to walk with me to his cottage?"

"I think I'll do a little more searching before it gets too dark."

I do, but I don't find the ring. Not that I ever stood a chance. If it was in the house, it's under tons of rubble. I put the metal detector up and wonder if I should go. I had hoped—stupidly, I guess—that I'd bump into Marchant, but since I didn't, I've got to decide if I feel brave enough to knock on his door.

Feeling like Little Red Riding Hood, I head back past the pool and pond, aiming toward the cottage I heard was his. As I walk through the oak grove, I see Loveless on her way back to the parking lot.

"How is he?" I ask.

She shrugs. "He didn't answer his doorbell."

"Oh. Well, have a safe trip."

"You too."

"It was nice meeting you." I'm surprised to find that's sort of true. I sit by the pond until she's gone, and then I stand up and watch the workers as they move about the cement truck. I'm not going to see him. Obviously. I was probably stupid to think I would. I should probably just go, but seeing how bad this place looks, learning that Marchant is probably in rehab, I feel compelled to leave a note.

I pull a notepad from my purse and write:

Marchant—
I'm sorry about what happened. I hope your re-building process is as quick and painless as possible.
Suri Dalton.

I'm tucking it into his door when it opens.

CHAPTER THIRTEEN

Marchant

I'M SHIRTLESS IN my most beat-up pair of khaki pants, and I'm in no state to talk to anybody, but once I get a glimpse of Suri Dalton, I can't help myself. I wrap my hand around the doorknob and look down on her through the window in my door. She's thoroughly fuckable in black shorts and a cream tank top.

My discharge paperwork says I claimed to have come from Suri Dalton's hotel room the night of my admission.

It probably isn't true. I have a memory of kissing her in the bathroom at the Wynn, but knowing what I know of her, I'm pretty sure she didn't fuck me the night of the fire.

The first thing I remember after walking out the ER's sliding glass doors is catching a ride with a woman on a motorcycle. She took me to The Deuce Longue, on The Strip, where I saw coverage of the Love Inc. fire on the news, got pissed off, and hit the bartender in the face. I don't remember any of that, but I have the police report. Apparently I told the cops I wasn't sure if I was really Marchant Radcliffe.

They asked me for ID, and I said I wanted a ride to the local morgue, because I was no one. They decided to take me to the hospital. When I arrived, I got a shot of sedatives and told someone to call Rachelle so she could verify that Love Inc. had not burned. Rachelle called Dr. Libby. We talked for a while, and I told her I stopped taking my Lithium weeks ago. March 15, to be exact. I woke up feeling like shit and I flushed it down the toilet. She understands why. She knows what that date means to me.

I stayed inpatient for five days, long enough to try ECT twice and decided I didn't like it enough to try it a third time. Long enough to get my medicine figured out and get me within a few days of Dr. Libby's return. Long enough to remember bits and pieces of what I can only assume was a fantasy.

I remember a mole on her belly. Does she really have a mole there?

I shouldn't open the door now, but I do. It's like fucking magic: Suri Dalton, flesh and blood, sharing air with me. She looks me over, head to toes, and frowns.

"Marchant...hi. I—" Her voice lilts a little and she blinks a few times. "I was here, looking for my grandmother's ring, which I didn't find, and I wanted to stop by and...bring you this." She holds a sheet of paper in front of my face. I read it once, then twice, so it sinks into my sluggish brain. "Speedy and painless..." I give her a tiny smile. "I'd drink to that." Except, of course, I'm back on the wagon.

She looks me over again. "How are you? You seem...tired."

I rub my eyes. "Yeah. Long day." I don't know what else to say. *Hi, I had ECT less than twenty-four hours ago and I can barely remember my middle name. Apparently sex with you was a key part of my psychotic delusion.*

I take the note. "Thanks." I let my eyes meet hers. "How'd you know I was here?"

"Lucky guess." She smiles, and it's so perfect I can feel an ache through the thick cloak of my medicine. I tap my fingers on my leg, and suddenly I feel illuminated. Like the blood is pumping through my body again. Like I'm alive. It takes me a moment to adjust, and when I do, I can't think of a single thing to say.

"Hunter wants to hear from you." Suri's thin brows scrunch

a little. "He's worried."

I hold out my arms. "Still kicking." Except I realize there are track marks on the inside of my elbows. And I'm probably giving her a good look at my tattoo. Fuck.

I scrub my hand back through my hair. "I'm fine," I tell her. I look down at a bowl on a table in my foyer. My housekeeper, Mrs. Everett, likes to fill it with Starburst—my favorite candy. I pluck out a red one and eat the damn thing in front of her. I don't know why. I'm nervous maybe.

"You doing okay?" I ask after I swallow.

"Can't complain." She runs her palm over her hair. "I'm flying back to Napa tomorrow."

I want her to stay, but that's delusional. Irrational. I have a hazy memory of something unpleasant going on between us in the hospital in El Paso when I was manic Marchant. I bet I was an asshole.

I force a smile. "I hope you have a good flight." Somewhere in the back of my mind, I feel like there's something else that I should say to her, but I can't think of it. They told me this was normal after ECT—memory problems; particularly problems with short-term memory. And for all that I hated the anesthesia IV and I hate the way it makes me feel like my insides were scooped out and there's nothing in me now, I'm not manic any-more.

I look down at my feet and then back up at her. I say the on-ly thing I can think of: "It was nice meeting you. You're a nice person."

"Thanks," she says, frowning.

And I want her to go now. I want her to go because I want to kiss her, and I don't like feeling out of control the way I do now that I am breathing her perfume.

She takes a small step back, and the vice around my throat loosens a little. And then her eyes widen. "Would it be okay if I used your bathroom? I'm so sorry to ask."

I can't tell her no, so I open the door a little wider and she comes inside.

Suri

HE LOOKS UNCOMFORTABLE. Unhappy. I remember how he hasn't been returning anyone's calls and how strung out he acted on the plane. I remember when that night at the hotel he told me not to ask if he was okay. Clearly, he's got…stuff. And I bet he wants to keep it private. So it's not surprising that he doesn't want me in his house. I wish I hadn't had to ask, but I'm a long way from the nearest gas station, and I chugged a big bottle of water on the way over here. Nerves, I guess.

He points me down a darkish hallway with stone floor and cream walls dotted with framed photos. I notice college-aged Hunter in a few of them, with college-aged Marchant.

"First door on the right," he calls behind me, and I wonder in what state I'll find the bathroom.

The bathroom door is tall and heavy—cherry wood with a crystal doorknob—and the half bath I step into is done in warm sage and cream, with a simple pedestal sink, an ordinary-looking toilet, a plush brown rug, and a rough woven basket that holds magazines. I lean over the magazine basket, expecting *Playboy* or *Hustler*, and I'm stunned to see *The New Yorker* and *Scientific American*. I glance up at the frame above the towel rack and am surprised to find myself staring down a Jack Kerouac quote.

"Suppose we suddenly wake up and see that what we thought to be this and that, ain't this and that at all?"

I make a surprised face at myself in the mirror over the sink and glance once at the door before sitting down to do my business. I get up quickly, wash my hands, and dry them on a small brown towel monogrammed with an "M."

As I blink into the mirror, I remember the lines of his beautiful torso—the mouth-watering body that's standing right down the hall. The way his weight felt against me on the bed. The way his mouth felt on my neck. The way his cock felt inside of me. And I can feel myself react.

This has never happened before. Ever—except that evening when I first met him in the Wynn.

I look into the mirror and my cheeks are pink. Pink like it's snowing outside and I have windburn. Pink like too long on the upper deck of a ship on a sunny day.

Before I leave the bathroom, I tell myself to calm down. He seems tired and kind of quiet today. Clearly, not in the mood for a repeat.

I wonder if he really went to rehab. He certainly seems more…settled somehow, now.

I take one more look at the framed quote on the wall and step back into the hall. My mind is spinning. The best thing to do would be to run—not walk—back to my rented Jeep and rely on my team of jewelry-finders to find Gran Gran's ring.

I'm glad I came and saw him, glad I wished him well, but I lose my head around this man. I'm losing it more now that I know he likes Kerouac.

Real pimps don't read good literature—do they?

I hurry down the hall and find him leaning against the wall at the mouth of the living area with his arms crossed. I can see the tattoo on his side, the mysterious date I remember from before.

He looks me over. His eyes are intense and slightly heavy. I can feel his attention on me like a laser, making me squirm.

"What's your favorite color?" he asks.

"Favorite color?"

He holds up a basket filled with Starbursts.

"Oh. I like the pinks."

"Good choice." He picks three pinks out and offers them too me. "For the road," he says.

"Thank you." That reminds me of the Kerouac quote.

I let my eyes have their way with his bare chest once more, willing him to respond. Willing him to take me to his bedroom. When nothing happens, I give up. I'm proud of myself for having the nerve to come out here, but it wasn't meant to be.

I take a step toward the door, and he moves with me. His eyes look a little brighter now; his body seems a little tenser.

"I like the reds," he says, "I'm an addict."

I'm not sure what to say to him. I'm almost to the door, but how do I say bye? I'm flipping through my list of possibilities when I feel his hand on my shoulder.

I turn toward him, struck again by how flipping hot he is without his shirt. Skin so smooth...every muscle flawless. And his eyes—those gorgeous brown eyes are honed on me.

"I...uh. I feel like I should be saying thank you for something. Something big. But I can't remember what it is. I don't...I can't remember much about the last week and a half. Fucking weird, I know." He moves his hand off my shoulder and rubs his head.

"You remember the night of the fire, don't you? The um...pool and everything?"

His face goes white. He blinks a few times. "I had forgotten that you pulled me out." His voice sounds low and very deep. His shoulders are visibly tense. I think he may be embarrassed.

Clearly, this confirms he has a drug problem.

"You don't have to say thank you. I would do it again in a heartbeat. I'm just happy I was there."

"Well anyway—thank you."

He turns around and grabs the basket. "Stay and let me pick out all the pinks?"

I'm surprised to feel my cheeks go hot. The way he's look-ing at me today…it's almost…sweet. Strangely, it makes him seem even hotter. I wonder briefly if his asshole moments were all because of drugs. If he doesn't remember the pool, does that mean he also forgot our night together? That would really suck.

I'm deep in thought when he interrupts with, "You're a de-signer, right? Interior decorating?"

I nod. "Yep." When he just keeps staring at me, I expound. "I own my own business in Napa." And, after a moment's hesita-tion, I decide to satiate my curiosity. "Did you use Sally Hurst when you opened?"

He nods. "Yeah. Fucking loved what she did with the place. She's moved to Greece now, but I guess you know that."

I do. "You should try Marianita Juarez."

He laughs. "I can't stand her."

"I see why." Marianita is just about as bossy as they come. She's good, but when she designs a space, she does it her way. I can't imagine Marchant Radcliffe would like that.

He steps a little closer, doing that thing again—the thing with his eyes. I feel like I'm being hypnotized, so at first it doesn't even register when he says, "I don't suppose you've got any openings."

I blink, shocked. "What kind of job?"

"You know…" He swipes his hand back through his hair. "The interior. Everything that burned. Possibly the other two buildings, too. So it all matches." He's staring at me earnestly. "I'd pay you well. Put you up in one of the cottages." He frowns. "I know that might not seem so good, but it won't be like before. No swimming," he jokes.

"What about sex?" I'm shocked when the question pops out of my mouth.

He's surprised, too. His eyebrows lift. "You want sex?"

"Maybe. I mean…yes. I think I would…like that."

"In lieu of payment?"

I laugh, even though I'm practically shaking with nervousness. "You're not that good."

His eyes narrow at that, and I think he's actually going to argue the point. Instead he says, voice all husky, "What if I can't stick to just once?"

"I don't know. I'm not interested in something…serious, but I think I might enjoy a few romps in the…hay." I smile a little, and feel like I might giggle, because I have no idea what I'm talking about. *BITE THE TONGUE! BITE THE—* okay. No giggles.

But I do tremble a bit when he steps even closer. "Romp implies something casual. Nothing about this will be casual. I don't have sex—I fuck. You understand?"

I nod. "Of course I do." Does *he* not? What kind of drugs was he doing that he forgot a whole night?

"So let me get this straight. You want to fuck me?"

I blush three shades of pink. "I know, I'm being blunt. It's not my usual style, but…yes."

"Think about this," he warns. "Whether you really want to be here, doing this with me. Because once you commit, you work on my terms."

"I understand." I just hope he doesn't walk out on me the way he did at the hotel. "I'll go back to the pent house for tonight and let you know tomorrow."

He's leaning out his doorway as I go. I already know my answer.

CHAPTER FOURTEEN

Marchant

I'VE JUST SWALLOWED my pills the next morning when I hear the knock. I wonder if it's Rachelle, coming back for something she forgot, but I get a tingly sixth sense as I stride toward the door. I look down at myself before moving for the knob. I'm wearing battered pajama pants and an equally battered grey undershirt. Suddenly it doesn't feel like enough. And it's not—because my sixth sense was correct. Through the small window at the top of the door, I see Suri Dalton.

She's gorgeous in a little yellow dress and strappy leather sandals. She's got on sunglasses I'm pretty sure are Ray-Bans. With her smooth, tanned skin and her pouty, bitable lips, she looks good enough to eat.

I tug the door open, feeling a little like the big, bad wolf. I don't usually fuck the women on my payroll, but this one came to me.

Still, my conscience stirs; it's Suri Dalton. She's beautiful and rich as sin—just about perfect, and she's throwing off an innocent vibe so strong I can practically smell it. I sort of feel like I'm bro-ing out trying to score with her; like back in my frat days, when the only kind of girl I wanted was the Sunday School Sorority Girl.

On the other hand, Suri Dalton *is* a grown woman who knows what she wants.

I'm not sure why I'm it—especially when I think about the few hazy things I *can* remember from the time we've spent together—but should I give a shit? I know I'd love to fuck her.

Not for long. No more than a week, and definitely no strings attached. That's my rule for life, because I would never ask anyone to share my baggage.

I can't be her friend, either. Too much attraction.

So let's say I'm taking her on out of curiosity—because I'm curious to see just what she wants from me.

I can already tell it's gonna suck when the hourglass runs out. I haven't been with any woman for more than a night—well, consecutively—in years. And Suri isn't just any woman.

I need to remind myself that this is about sex. She probably sees me as sex personified—she wouldn't be the first—and wants to pop her stranger-fucking cherry. And I *am* a stranger to her, thank God. She pulled me from the pool and that's all. There's no record of her at the hospital with me. She didn't see my pitiful state. She sees me as sex.

I peer down at her, already getting hard.

She smiles—a wholesome, winning smile. "I'll do it. I mean, I'll take the job."

"I was hoping you'd say that."

I think I see a light blush on her cheeks as she shifts her weight from one sandaled foot to the other. "I don't have to start today necessarily. In fact, I probably need to go home for a few days and get some of my things. But I wanted to let you know my decision. Also, I'm meeting a team here in about an hour to show them where to look for my grandmother's ring. I lost it…that night. Which is why I saw the pool," she tacks on quietly.

I nod. What she means is, that's how she found me at the bottom of the pool. This morning when I woke up, I remembered a little bit more. Shivering. Getting sick. Feeling like I couldn't breathe.

Damnit, I'm a mess. I *was* a mess. I tell myself that shit's behind me now. I can go back to life the way it used to be. Quiet and solitary; responsible living with the occasional quick fuck. Never anything serious.

And never with anyone who hits me like she does.

I look her over, floored by how fresh and clean she looks. Like sunshine. She tucks a strand of her short, brown-blond hair behind her ear, looking a little uncomfortable, as if she can sense my scrutiny. I offer her a small smile. "Do you want some coffee? Waffles?"

I'm feeling more clear-headed today, so my heart pounds slightly as I wait for her answer. It's strange; nerves. Like I'm a 15-year-old virgin again. I had my first post-hospital boner this morning, and it was all for her. The fantasy of sweet Suri, sucking my cock with a cherry red condom on it.

"Sure," she says finally. "I'd like that."

I swing the door open. "Come on in."

I think about my house as she follows me through the open living area into the kitchen. Most people who see the place are surprised by how cozy it is. Two fluffy couches in the den, a big, oak chifferobe to hide my flatscreen. Built-in shelves filled with books and other shit I hang onto. The funniest thing: Unlike the main house and the other two manor houses, I decorated this place myself. And I don't go for that sleek, shiny shit like Hunter does. I like to be comfortable.

The kitchen is done in various shades of brown and beige and wood, with a deep red, cherrywood breakfast table. I'm not much of a cook, but I like to try sometimes, so I've got pots and skillets hanging above a small island.

I've already got the waffle mix whipped up, because now that I'm mostly just back to my Lithium, I expect to be hungrier. I need the weight if I'm going to get back to the gym. And I am.

I need the work outs to keep me level.

I pull out a chair for Suri Dalton, and she sits in one elegant motion. She looks up at me, smiling like I've done something funny. "You cook," she says. "Like Hunter. I'm surprised."

I laugh at that as I move around the kitchen. "No. Bro can cook. I just fuck around in the kitchen."

"That looks like a real waffle iron to me."

"Rachelle," I say, and belatedly realize she doesn't know what that means. "She won this at a charity raffle. The one she had at home was nicer, so she gave it to me." I wave in a kind of general way around the kitchen. "I get a lot of her castoffs."

"Sounds nice." At first I think she might be sarcastic, but when I look up at her, she seems sincere. I wonder if she likes to cook, but I won't ask.

I pour some batter into the iron and prep two plates with some fruit Rachelle actually did cut and bring over.

"Milk, Orange juice, or apple?" I ask her as I close the iron and turn to the refrigerator.

"Apple, thanks."

I pour her juice, plus some water for myself, and glance over at her as she sits there watching me, all prim and pretty. Prim doesn't really do her justice, though. She's not *prim*. She's more like...put-together. Neatly put-together and kind of...elegant.

She leans forward over the table, distracting me from my thoughts with a hint of cleavage. "So I want to know some more about you. Now that you're my client and all. And I'd like to know a little bit about the history of this place."

My chest squeezes as I think about all the shit that burned. The cheesy, framed first dollar that I made. The ribbon from our ribbon-cutting at the original brothel, on the Strip. A bunch of pictures of escorts who've worked here. I wish I wasn't so fuck-ing sentimental.

The waffle hisses a little, so I open the iron and drop it out onto a plate. I'm buttering the thing when I realize I'm not sure how she likes it, and anyway...didn't she ask me something? I gather the syrup and the butter, plus some silverware, and try to remember what she asked. I feel better today—more like me—but I'm still kind of foggy.

I set the plate down in front of her, set the silverware where it should go, and turn around to grab a napkin.

Oh...*the ranch*! And me, I think wryly.

I turn back to her with my best poker face. "The truth is, I always did like orgies, so I decided to form my own personal harem."

I watch her heart-shaped face carefully, focusing on her eyes, because I expect them to get wide. She holds her cards close, though, so the only way I know that she's unsure of whether to believe me is the tiny twitch at the side of her mouth.

"Really, though," she says, pouring syrup over her waffle, "how does one decide to be a pimp?"

"I'm not a pimp," I tell her. "I consider myself a business man, but if that doesn't sit well with you, think of me as a mack."

Now her eyes narrow: hazel, framed by long, thick lashes, topped by thin, elegant brows. "What's a mack?"

I drop down into the seat across from her and rest my fore-arms on the table. "A mack works for the girl. Keeps her—or in my case, her and him—safe. Makes sure clients pay up. A pimp makes sure the escort pays up. Rents her out." I shake my head. "Everybody who works here wants to, and they make a fuck lot of money doing it."

Suri considers this as she chews her waffle, then smiles up at me. Her smile is so damn sweet. I want to kiss her. "I can maybe accept that," she says. "And I love the waffle. You *do* cook."

"Maybe?" I smirk. "Do I look like a pimp to you?"

She laughs as she looks me up and down. "I think the waffle

iron might have pushed you more into the mack camp."

"I'm a mack. I'm telling you." She licks her lip and I get up from the table. I'll never lose my boner if I don't put some distance between us. I angle my body so she can't see me from the front, then hide behind part of the counter as I pour more batter into the waffle iron that's resting on my little island.

I look over my shoulder at her. "One of my chick friends in college was a stripper. Never had good bosses, always got a bunch of shit. She told me it was better out in Vegas, or at least that's what she heard. With it being legal and all, there are rules. A lot of rules," I say dryly. "I was majoring in business and English, and I thought it sounded like a decent idea. A different kind of brothel. Classy. Clean. Safe. Hunter fronted me the money." I don't tell her how I also invested most of my parents' life insurance. I don't like to talk about my parents.

"Turned out—" I tap my head— "I've got a head for business. And I try to make it a fun work environment."

"Selling their bodies for sex?" She dabs her mouth with a napkin. "No offense, but how can you make that a fun experience?"

I shrug. "Healthcare. Movie Nights. A movie theatre. Security. Free iPhones. They screen their own clients and accept or decline whoever they like. At least at the ranch they do. The Strip location works more like a typical brothel—mostly a bunch of bachelor parties and high school dudes and basement dwellers stepping out from behind a game console for a few hours." I throw a sidelong glance at her and wink. "I've even got a company shrink out here. A gym, sauna, salon. It's not such a bad place."

She gives me an unreadable look, and I shake my head. "And still, the lady doth protest."

"It's not that." She shrugs one bare shoulder. "I just think it's weird."

"It is, I guess. But it's a service that's in demand. That's not changing."

"It's made you a good living," she says thoughtfully.

Yeah, it has, but I shrug. "I guess."

"Do you enjoy it?" she asks before biting a strawberry in half.

"I do, mostly. It's a lot like running a hotel—or at least I imagine it is. You've gotta focus on the client. The experience."

Her cheeks redden at the word *experience*, and it hits me like a fucking asteroid. I remember *everything*. Suri's face inside the ambulance. Suri at the hospital. I remember pulling her into my hotel room and—

"Jesus Christ." I wheel around, leaning on the island, and grab my head. My legs feel weak. For a moment, it's a struggle just to breathe.

"Marchant? Are you okay?" She's on her feet. Probably about to come over here. I can't take it, so I whirl around. "I'm fine," I snap. "Sit down."

Oh, fuck. I fucked Suri Dalton—fucked her hard—and I left her there alone. I rub my face and flinch when I smell the waffle burning. I pull it out and toss it on a plate.

I turn to her. "Why are you here?" I snarl. "Are you stupid? Or do you like being treated like a whore?"

Her mouth drops, and her face reddens. She's shocked, angry, insulted. "I thought it would be a fun job. Is that a problem? What is wrong with you?"

"Why do you want to sleep with me again?"

"I want to fuck you," she corrects.

"Fuck." What's wrong with her? I tug at my hair.

"You're acting weird. Like you're pissed. Was that another thing that you forgot?" She looks disappointed.

I don't address that—the part about me forgetting. I figure I look crazy enough without confirming her suspicions. "Not pissed. Fucking confused. What about that night appealed to you? What made you want to do that again?"

"…I don't know," she murmurs. She's looking down at her perfect manicure. Her eyes collide with mine. "I wanted to get to know you more, I guess. The attraction—the chemistry— It's clearly there. Don't try to say it's not, because I won't believe it. You didn't treat me like a whore. We had rough sex, which I liked." She shrugs. "Anyway, why are you asking all these questions now?"

"What does it matter?" I snap.

"Marchant," she says gently, "do you have a drug problem?"

"Did I tell you that I did?"

Her eyes widen. "Are you trying to confuse me?"

"No. I'm not. I'm sorry." I squeeze my eyes shut and lean against the island again. God, I need to get myself together. I stand up straight and turn to face her. "Suri…I think this is a bad idea. You being here."

"But you're the one who—"

"I know, but look—I changed my mind."

She's up from the table in an instant. Her hair falls in layers around her face, and her hazel eyes look red and watery. "Was it that bad?"

"No. Jesus, no. Not at all. I don't remember very clearly, but I don't need to. You're goddamn beautiful and I'm just sorry that I left you there."

"You have a drug problem," she says slowly.

"Yes," I tell her grimly, hoping this will send her on her way. I open my mouth to tell her I'm a wicked bastard—good for no one. Just ask Marissa.

"Were you in rehab recently?"

"I was," I say.

"So you were on drugs that night? The night of the fire?"

"Yes," I lie. A drug problem is better than a mental problem, isn't it?

"And now you're clean?"

"That's none of your business," I tell her.

"I'm sorry. I'm not trying to be nosey. I just…want to help."

It's something about that. Something about the way her face goes soft and caring. I just can't take it.

"If you stay, you stay on my terms."

"We already said that. Yesterday. I'm fine with that."

My frustration multiplies. I wave at the door. "Go. Find someone else." This won't be the emotionless fuck-fest I'd imagined for us. Not now that I know she saw me sniveling about needles. Not when she saw me getting all teary on the bed at the hotel because the smooth lines of her soft body reminded me of Marissa.

"Go," I tell her. "I don't want you here."

She walks close to me, so close I can smell her syrupy breath. She runs a finger over my lip, and I go so still.

"I don't believe you."

"Stupid," I say.

I lift her in my arms to carry her to the door. Because I'm humiliated. Because I feel something for her—because she saw me in that state and she came back.

Halfway across the den, she wraps her arms around my neck and rests her forehead on my chest. I divert toward my bedroom.

CHAPTER FIFTEEN

Suri

AS HE SPIRITS me across his den and down a long, dark, hardwood hall, my mind spins. Marchant Radcliffe has a drug problem. He doesn't remember having sex with me. He just offered to make me feel used—then begged me to go. And now he's carrying me into his room.

The bed is big—king-sized with engraved mahogany posts and crimson bedding. I notice long, dark curtains and a vast bookshelf before he yanks the duvet back and drops me on the satiny sheets.

He grabs the hem of my dress and tugs it toward my head. "I warned you. I told you to go—but you didn't, did you?"

I hold up my arms and feel the whoosh of the dress over my head. All I'm wearing underneath it is a yellow thong and matching lacy bra. I stare up at him as he sets his mouth in a scowl, his biceps rippling as he pulls off his own t-shirt and tosses it behind him. He leans over me and fingers a strand of my hair.

"You're here because you want to be fucked."

I nod, because those eyes of his are liquid brown and hot as fire, and I'm mesmerized.

He rolls me over on my side, making quick work of my bra. My breasts bounce free as he rolls me back onto my back, but he's already moving lower, licking down my belly as he shoves my thong aside and thrusts a finger into me. He covers my pussy with his mouth and I moan.

"I'm gonna give you what you want," he pants against my thigh.

His tongue flicks hard against my clit, and my orgasm is almost violent, making me convulse and cry out, "Marchant!"

He takes a step back and drops his plaid pajama pants. His dick springs out. It's big and hard and standing tall—for me.

I sit up, leaning closer to him. He thinks he's in charge here, but he's going to have to learn to share the power. "I made that happen," I murmur. I never felt this…sexy with Adam, and I feel elated. "Do you want to use me, Marchant?"

I press my breasts together.

"Do you like having sex with sluts?" I ask him in my most sultry voice. "Is that why you're a mack—because you like the girls?" He's panting now, and I grin wickedly. "I can be your whore."

His nostrils flare, his eyes are flooded with lust, and I grin again, tweaking my nipples. "Bring that cock to me."

He's on the bed before I draw my next breath, pushing me down on my back and straddling my belly. "Taste it," he says. "Swallow it."

My heart is beating hard as he shoves himself into my mouth. He thrusts gently at first, and then a little harder—but never too hard. I swirl my tongue around him, opening wider so I can take in all of him. I'm surprised to find I really love this. I cup my palm around his balls and twirl my tongue around his head and pump my hand near the base of his cock. His hands come down harder on my shoulders.

"Yes, that's right. Yes."

And I'm secretly thrilled when he tightens and I can feel him on the verge—until he pulls away.

"What—"

He has me flat on my back in a millisecond. He leans over,

producing a condom maybe from a nightstand drawer—but it seems like thin air. He rolls it over his thick length, spreads my legs, and looks into my eyes.

"Are you ready?"

I nod, and he impales me.

I lose the capacity to breathe as pleasure surges through me. My legs are limp. My feet tremble. My stomach quivers. And in between my legs, I'm stretched full, bursting; hot and tight and roaring. Then he starts to move, and I am screaming.

Sex has never felt like this. Like we're one person—two halves of a whole. I rock my hips, arching off the mattress because I am desperate—aching—for more of him. Above me, leaning on sinewy arms, Marchant's eyes are wide open. He's watching me—watching my every groan.

"Tell me you like it," he purrs.

"I love it."

"Tell me that you want me deeper." I lift my hips as he thrusts deeper in.

"I want you deeper," I cry hoarsely.

And then he angles himself just so, so the base of him slides slickly over my aching, swollen clit, and I roll over the edge with an animal roar.

It's not until sometime later, when the buzzing in my head is quiet and my body has stopped glowing, that I realize he must have come when I did. He's lying on his side, the condom gone, his cock still long and mostly hard, his chest within licking range, wearing a Cheshire cat grin. He looks gorgeous enough to stop hearts.

"Oh my God." I'm panting. I realize suddenly that I'm spread out, totally nude, and grope for a blanket—but the covers are thrown off the mattress, hanging down onto the floor. "Damnit. You're a Beast in bed. I mean…whoa."

"Best you've ever had?" His smile widens just a little.

"Yes."

"You were pretty good yourself. Passionate. We fit together well."

I smile. "I think so." I'm about to confess that I've never done anything like this before when he leans forward, looking into my eyes with his dark ones.

"I enjoyed this so much that I've changed my mind. You can stay here—if you want to. You'll stay until we've run this dry and then, if you're not finished with the job, I'll go. To one of my other houses. Does that sound like a deal?"

I nod. I don't see where I can go wrong, and even if I can, after the sex we just had, I'm not sure it's possible for me to turn him down. "Sounds good to me."

"There's only one thing you need to keep in mind, and that is: this is just sex. I'm not in the market for a relationship." He says the word as if it's something dangerous. "If you find yourself developing…feelings, or, in fairness, if I do…I can go."

"Where?" The question just pops out.

"I have a cabin in Wyoming." Before I can comment, he's rising up off the bed, slipping into a robe I didn't even see him grab. "Do you agree to let me know?" he asks. "If you find yourself wanting more than sex?"

I sit up, glancing around the plush rug for my own discarded clothes. "I do."

"Then lie back down."

He takes my shoulders gently, easing me down onto my back, and spreads my legs again.

Marchant

I'M WEAK.

So fucking weak.

I should have tossed her out the door, but I had to take her to my room. And fuck her. And find that, just like last time, she fit perfectly around my cock.

I rub my eyes and tell myself I won't let it get personal; she already knows I don't want this to get personal. No getting to know her, and definitely no letting her know me. I'll give her perimeters for the job and let her at it, and when she's got down time, I'll fuck her senseless. The sex is as much a part of our deal as the contract she's signing at Rachelle's cottage right now for the design job. I remind myself that it, too, is business. A cock and a cunt. Nothing but biology.

Except that as I showed her out the door, I had a vivid memory of her eyes. They were unhappy. So was her mouth, and that's because she was talking to a nurse in the ER. She was talking on my behalf—talking about needles.

Next I remember watching from across a hotel lobby as she passed her credit card across the desk. Which led me full-circle, since earlier today, my memory of our hotel room encounter returned.

I fucked Suri Dalton—manic as sin; out of my damn mind. I fucked her hard. And then I left her there. I'm not sure what bothers me so much about that. I've done the same with other women—just taken off, with no explanations and no apologies—but it does. And it's triggering as hell to know I fucked her while I was manic. Triggering because it reminds me of Marissa.

So today, I was a little rough with her. Damn right. I wanted to drive her off, and if not—*obviously* not—I wanted to show her

I'm not like her Adam. Not like Carlson, or any other man she might have climbed in bed with. I don't want a relationship. I don't want her heart and soul, and I damn sure don't need saving. Not right now, anyway. The only reason she's still here is I could use a few good fucks to chase away the remnants of my darkness.

HALF AN HOUR later, I'm feeling steady again. I'm watching something on the Science channel, still glowing my post-fuck glow, when I get a text from Juniper: *'Mr. Obar coming this evening. Which cottage?'*

A quick call to Rachelle, another call to my grounds manager, and shit! I'm out of cottages.

I put Juniper in the rear room of a cottage Leslie is using, and work on pacing a hole in my floors. Suri Dalton will be back with her bags in a few days, and there's nowhere for her to stay.

I call Rachelle once more, just to confirm the grim news—but I'm correct. Stacy returned from a brief vacation and is taking clients in a cottage with Alicia, while the third cottage across the yard is closed because of sewerage issues. Which means the only spare room on the whole damn premises is inside my place.

I'm not sure I can stand to be so close to her. If I'm honest with myself, I guess I just find it…fucking weird that she wants anything to do with me. I mean, yeah, I'm in pretty decent shape and I'm not too tough on the eyes. But she pulled me out of a fucking pool.

I guess objectively, that's not too weird. Not unless you know what I know: that I drowned that night on purpose. Because without Lithium, I do that sort of thing.

I'm wondering if I can keep my shit together, wondering if I can share my space with her and keep my secrets tucked away, when I get a text. I slide the lock key on my phone, wondering for a moment if maybe she's canceling. But it isn't her.

The first clue it's something strange is that it comes from an unknown number.

I open the text, wondering if I gave my number to any of the escorts I ordered after getting back from El Paso. I don't remember them, but my bank statement does.

What greets me makes my head feel too light. Like a balloon that just might float away.

"You going to pay me, or should I take down something dearer to you than your precious whore house?"

I lie down on the couch and stare up at my ceiling. Then, instead of calling Suri Dalton, telling her not to come back, I call my money guy.

I give him Hawkins' bank account number, the one my P.I., David, dug up, and have him deposit the amount I owe, plus twenty-five percent. I'm not sure anymore what's dear to me, but I'm not taking chances.

CHAPTER SIXTEEN

Suri

AFTER I LEAVE Marchant's cottage, I have coffee with Rachelle and her partner, meet the team of gem-finders I hired to find Gran Gran's ring, and take a quick flight back to Napa.

I spend three days getting the house in order, collecting my "toolbox" full of fabric and textile samples I think would interest Marchant, and lying low.

Most of the lying low is because of Adam and Brina. My sisters have given me the heads up that Brina is parading Adam all over town, and the last thing I need is a run-in with the two of them. I'm ashamed to admit, I'm hiding from Lizzy, too. Because once she knows I took the Love Inc. job, she'll know about Marchant and me. I just know she will.

When she texts me the first day I'm home, I tell her I'm chin-deep in a new project and need to talk later. When she calls the second day, we talk for half an hour, focused completely on how she and Hunter are dealing with the pregnancy. (Hunter is playing the part of nurse but not saying much about the baby, which is fine at the moment because Lizzy has just started getting morning sickness).

I spend the third day at Crestwood Place cleaning. I'm kind of a neat-freak, and I can't leave the house without cleaning it. I'm feeling even tidier than usual because moving around helps me avoid dwelling on Marchant. Not that I don't want to think about him. Because I do. I just don't want to *dwell*.

Finally, it's go time.

The plane is in the air just a few minutes after ten on Monday morning. I spend the flight jotting down design ideas and indulging a rare classical music mood with a little Chopin.

The CRV I rented this time is white and waiting for me at the little private airport about twenty minutes from the ranch. I stop by a little grocery store before heading toward Love Inc., still feeling good about things.

But by the time my grocery-laden Jeep is bouncing down a ribbon of freshly paved county road, it's mid-afternoon, and I don't feel relaxed. My heart kicks into an erratic rhythm as I turn onto an even smaller drive. As I follow it through a grove of trees, toward a small, square parking lot, I try to convince myself that I took this job for personal reasons. Because I need a few weeks to lie low. Because it'll be nice to get out of my big, lonely Crestwood Place for a little while. Because the job will look good on my resume.

I see a swatch of stone through brush—one of the cottages—and my stomach knots, because I know I'm lying to myself. I'm here because Marchant Radcliffe offered me the job. I'm here because, despite all logic, I enjoy sex with him.

He's obviously got problems, but when I'm kissing him, I don't think about anything but him. I don't worry. I don't feel lonely or sad. In a way, *he* is like *my* drug. His skin and his scent. I like the way he moves, the way he speaks. He intoxicates me, and like an addict, I'm parking my CRV and opening the door because I'm back for more.

It's not just his body that intrigues me. I want to know his secrets, too. What does that tattoo mean? Why the drug problem? I want to fix him. And that's not just stupid, it's reckless. Yet I'm hoisting my duffel bag onto my shoulder, scooping up bags of groceries. Walking down the little pebble path that leads from this discreet parking lot to the row of cottages. To his cottage.

It's my choice. I can choose to be stupid if I want to be.

Before I see his cottage, I see the main house, and whoaaaaa. During my breakfast with Rachelle the morning I was here last, when she told me the main house would be built in under a month, I didn't believe her.

But...whoa. I'm not construction site-savvy, but I've worked on a few new builds with clients, and there have to be at least five crews working on this building. And what they've done in four days! There are walls now. Scaffolding walls, but walls nonetheless. Stone is piled high around the newly resurrected building skeleton; stone and shingles and shutters.

Marchant's place is on the end of the row of cottages—the one that's closest to the pond and the new "main house" at Love Inc. As soon as my eyes hit the front door, my pulse goes crazy and I start to sweat.

I tell myself this can't end badly. He's a pimp. I could never fall in love with a man like him. But I can have fun. And I'm overdue for some fun.

Marchant meets me on his porch. He's wearing dark slacks and a white shirt. His face sports stubble that's making its way into a beard. His eyes are sharp. I can feel him look me over. Can literally feel the heat.

I smile a little, but his lips don't curl at all. He looks...like a hungry tiger. It's a long moment before he takes the groceries from me. Our bodies brush, and I have a hard time making my legs carry me through the door he pushes open for me.

"Let's put your groceries in here," he says. "I've got the contractor waiting for us so we can talk about the timetable."

I watch the way his back ripples under his shirt as he puts my orange juice, butter, milk, and eggs into his wide stainless steel refrigerator. I watch the way his strong hands flex as he lets go of the other bags, leaving them lined up on his counter.

"I'm excited to meet him—or her."

"Him," he tells me, leading the way back to the front door. He's walking slightly fast, a step ahead of me; when he looks at me, he's glancing over his shoulder. I get the strange sense that he's wound up. Slightly tense. Is it possible I'm making him as antsy as he makes me? With his history, it seems doubtful. But still, I entertain the idea as I follow him out onto his porch and stand behind him while he locks the door.

I watch him slide the key into his pocket, noting the small, manatee keychain, and when he turns to me, our gazes collide. I take a small step back. A second passes as he seems to collect himself.

"Shall we?" He nods at the construction site two or three hundred yards through the trees, and I say, "Sure."

We walk close together, shoulders and elbows bumping once or twice. Past the pond. Past the grove of trees. He tells me about the construction crew—one big crew that typically does big, casino-style jobs—and the timeline as we move within sight of the pool.

He's saying something about, "Tom, the main guy," and how his last project was a dog track, but I'm not really listening. I'm imagining him on the concrete, shirtless and pale. I have a strange memory of myself, lying on my back, choking on blood beside my own pool. March 15. I wonder for the jillionth time what that date means to him.

"Suri?"

"Yes?"

He's standing in front of me. He puts his hands on my shoulders. "Don't think about that."

I feel a blush cross my cheeks. "How did you know?"

"You look like someone just killed your kitten."

I scrunch my nose. "I'm more a dog person."

"Then puppy," he says.

Behind him, men and women move about the cement and plywood site, but all I see are those brown eyes. Hypnotic eyes.

Heat flows from his palms, through my blouse, into my shoulders, spreading downward. I can barely find the words to reply, "That's not how I look."

"It is," he tells me softly. "Don't."

There's a hint of something stern in his voice—almost harsh. A warning? Don't make this into more than what it is, he's saying.

"I won't." I toss my hair—to…what? To show him that I'm not getting too serious about all this.

"I mean it," he whispers. "I want you to forget about that. Forget everything that happened before right now. If you need help," he says with a smug look, "I'll help you when we're done here."

I'm so rattled I can barely manage a nod. A few seconds later, a tall African-American man strides over with his gloved hand outstretched. Tom.

We spend the next half hour walking the site, with Marchant introducing me to his construction crew and me asking questions. I discuss some of my ideas, little things to make the original design a little cozier, a little sexier, and Tom tells us how long it would take to make them happen. Since the escorts' dormitory building also got damaged, it's being gutted and expanded slightly, with new suites carved out for the girls (and guys). For coordination purposes, the building on the right, the one with the library, salon, doctor's office, and whatever else is there, will be getting new décor as well.

By the time our conversation with Tom is over, I've decided I'll probably be here at least three weeks. Maybe four. And I feel giddy. Middle school crush giddy.

The feeling quickly dissipates, leaving cold anticipation as we walk back through the grove. He feels it, too. I can tell. And I think it's just sexual tension—same as what I feel—until we reach his door and he turns to me. "Suri…there's been a change. You'll be staying here with me."

Marchant

I WATCH HER eyes widen. Pretty eyes. She looks startled.

"If that doesn't work, there's a decent hotel about seven miles away. I can book you there."

The sun is going down, casting a red sheen over her face. I can't tell what she's thinking. But I'm on edge, waiting for her answer.

She smiles. "You don't have to do that. I'm okay here. But where will you stay?"

"I've got a suite downstairs in the basement."

"Oh." She nods. "That sounds fine. Did you run out of rooms?"

"Something like that."

"Are you sure you don't mind? I could do the hotel if that's easiest."

"No—you're fine."

I lead her inside and wave toward my room. "I've got another bedroom by my room, but it's kind of bare bones. My room is yours if you want it."

I watch the uncertainty flit across her face, followed by a long look into my eyes. She's trying to see what I want, but I keep my face neutral. I want to see if she'll take the lead.

"Um, okay. If you're sure?"

I like the way she hesitates. Polite. I don't see that often in Vegas.

"I wouldn't want it any other way," I tell her, as I step to the couch where I sat her bag. I throw it over my shoulder and lead her down the hall. Turn on the light to my room. It's large, with a bed, a bookshelf, a dresser, and a couch.

Truth is, I don't like being in it. Not after the last few weeks. I need a break. And there's something good about seeing her in it. I have the preposterous thought that the room deserves an occupant like her—to sort of clear out the bad vibes. But that's just fucking stupid.

"Bathroom's in here," I say, opening that door. "I already got my stuff out. Just use what you want."

She gives the bathroom an appreciative glance—it's large, and done to the nines—and I realize I left my medicine in the medicine cabinet. Stupid!

No—wait. Rachelle has it. Because no one trusts me.

Which leads me to remember I need to go see Libby. Soon.

I surprise even myself by grabbing Suri Dalton around the waist and tossing her onto my bed. Pulling down her pants and eating her pussy. She's screaming by the time I'm done, and I'm laughing, because really, I do enjoy eating her pussy.

I lick my lips and scoop the TV remote off a bedside table, toss it her way. Walk over to the wall and press the button that brings the TV down from the ceiling.

"Wow," she giggles, pointing the remote at the screen.

I arch my eyebrows. "I'll be back in a little while. You eat meat?"

That earns me a laugh. "Yes. I eat meat—when I'm in the mood." Another giggle, followed by a palm-muffled, "I'm sorry. I'm not usually quite so weird."

If this is weird I don't even wanna know what she would call me.

"There's a TV guide if you press the round, blue button. I'll be back in an hour."

I saunter down the hall feeling oddly light, despite where I'm going.

CHAPTER SEVENTEEN

Suri

"OKAY, YOU SAID not to say it, but I've gotta say it. Suri, I think the odds are really good that you have lost your mind. Like…really lost it. Or maybe been abducted by aliens. Is that what happened? You're the freakish, robotic, sex-obsessed—"

I squeak. "C'mon, Lizzy! No! This is not about sex."

She laughs. "Don't lie to me."

"I'm not lying!"

"And that's how I know you are. Your voice goes up and gets all squeaky, and—"

"It's not! It's not about sex! It's about…freedom."

She laughs even louder. "Being free to be Marchant's little bunny?"

"Is that why they call it the fluffy bunny ranch? I thought bunnies were Playboy."

Lizzy snorts. "There are actual bunnies, Suri. Look outside."

"Are you kidding?"

"No, I'm really not."

I frown at the phone. "How did I miss that?"

"I have no idea."

"Hmmmm…I'm not sure I believe you."

"I know I don't believe you! You've had sex with him. I

157

can hear it in your voice. And it's okay—really, I'm the last person on earth to have an opinion about that. But…seriously, Suri, be careful. Marchant is… He's Marchant. He's done a lot of not smart things lately and I just don't want to see you caught up in that."

I cross my legs. I'm sitting on his cozy couch, staring at his bed. "I'm not getting attached. Cross my heart and hope to die. This is just a fling, you know? Something fun."

"You need something fun." See? This is why Lizzy is my BFF.

"So Hunter is…better?" I ask her. "He seems to be adjusting?"

"Sort of. I mean…he's being really nice, and he hasn't left or called off the wedding or anything—"

"I knew he wouldn't!"

"But he's not himself."

"Like how?"

"Just not himself. It's hard to explain. Trust me. He is being weird. But he is still here, and so I'm hoping we can work out…all the other."

"You guys are like salt and pepper."

"Salt and pepper?" Lizzy says. "Wasn't that a band when we were in elementary school?"

"Cinnamon and sugar?" I offer.

"Yep," she says. "Like cinnamon and sugar."

We talk for a few more minutes, during which she urges me to befriend some of the women here, and during which I ask if she knows what Marchant's tattoo means.

"I didn't even know he had a tattoo," she says. But she promises to ask Hunter.

I hang up feeling strangely satisfied. Then I hear the front door open.

Marchant

I'M LOOKING FOR the Adobo seasoning when she walks into the kitchen. I can feel her standing there, looking at me, and I don't like it.

I wish I'd never volunteered to make burgers. I did offer to make burgers, didn't I? Now I can't even remember what I said to her.

It's like going to talk to Dr. Libby took me back four days. I feel like I can't fucking think straight. I feel like shit.

"You're going to have a lot of ups and downs in your life. That's normal for everyone." That's what she told me.

But it's bullshit. Nothing about me is normal. I did a good job of hiding that for fucking years, but then it fucking fell apart.

I'm not normal, and I don't belong around people who are.

I don't mean in matters of business.

Or maybe I do. I'm used to thinking I do a damn good job with this place, but I fucking burned it to the ground this time. Literally. Someone could have died, and it would have been my fault. Someone could have died because I don't belong around normal people. Not even in business. Especially not when it comes to business.

Maybe I should tell Suri Dalton to go. Maybe I should sell this fucking place.

"Marchant?"

I stare at the cabinets in front of me, wondering where the fuck I keep my spices. I need to season the patties on the pan in front of me, but I don't remember where I keep my spices. Because I'm not normal. Normal people don't sacrifice a slice of their memory to get their mind back in order. Normal people don't have to do that.

I wish, for a long moment, that I remembered even less than what I do. That I remembered nothing.

The tattoo on my side tingles.

Libby wanted to talk about that today, too, but I said no. No fucking way. I can't go there.

"Um, Marchant?"

I turn around, ready to snap her head off, but I get one long look at her and I just can't. Her hair's all smooth and shiny, and she's wearing another one of those goddamned dresses. This one is plain looking, and kind of peach-ish colored. It fits her curves just right, outlining her small, pert tits, and I can see her bare legs from the thighs down. Her toenails are painted pale purple. I want to suck them. Instead, I drag my eyes back to her face and mutter, "What?"

"Um, hi." She gives a little wave and smiles in a way that makes me feel unsteady. "What's up?"

I blink a few times, trying to clear my head so I don't look like a dumbass. "Just working on dinner." I feel awkward as hell. I mean, really. What am I, her husband?

"Are those burgers behind you?"

"Yep."

"Would you like some help? Chopping tomatoes or washing the lettuce or something?"

I rub my face, because I still feel half asleep and foggy. I don't need her help, don't even know if I want her close to me. But I say, "Yeah, why not."

I pull a chopping board from a cabinet, a knife from a drawer, and a head of lettuce and a few tomatoes from the refrigerator. "There ya go."

I turn back to the burgers, and I finally remember I keep seasoning in the cabinet closest to the refrigerator. That loosens me up a little, so I start to hum before I realize I probably sound off-key. I don't have a good voice. Never have.

"So, the site has come a long way," she says.

I look over at her; she's standing on the other side of the oven, looking up at me through a strand of her pretty brown-blonde hair.

"Umm. Yeah." Fuck me. I try again, hoping to pass as human this time, but all I sound is terse when I say: "It's coming along."

"Bad afternoon?"

I blink at her.

"I'm sorry. I didn't mean to pry, but you seem kind of like you had a rough day."

I do? Of course I fucking do. I run my fingers through my hair: my go-to gesture when I'm about to lose my shit; one that no doubt makes me look like the strung out junkie I led her to believe I am. I heave a deep breath and cut my eyes her way. "You probably shouldn't be staying here."

"I shouldn't?" Her hazel eyes widen just a little.

I shake my head. "I don't share space well, and I don't like making small talk."

She opens her mouth, and a big, hot rush of guilt spreads through me. "I'm sorry," I say. "That was really fucking rude." I find myself telling her, "I had a shitty day, okay? I don't want to talk about it. And thanks for your help with the—" I wave at the small spread of tomato slices out in front of her— "condiments or whatever."

Condiments isn't the right word, and that bothers me. Specificity is a thing I've always valued, and I can't be specific because I can't remember words I'm looking for.

The ECT was a bad decision. One I only made because...I wanted to forget my fuck ups. Naturally, I remember all my painful secrets clearly, and what I don't remember is my way around the kitchen.

I season the patties while an uncomfortable silence fills the space. I steal glances at her hands to see the moment when she's finished cutting tomatoes. When she is, I say, "There's a TV over there by the table. Why don't you turn it on and find something to watch? I'll finish this."

If she thinks anything of my suggestion, she doesn't say so. She just sits the knife down on the edge of the chopping block and gives me a neutral-looking sort-of-smile before walking over to the small TV stand beside my dining table and turning on the TV. She sits down in that way she does things: elegant and smooth, like, I guess, the kind of girl she is. She flips channels while I finish seasoning the burgers and walk outside to my waiting grill.

CHAPTER EIGHTEEN

Suri

I'M PRETTY DECENT at being discreet with my emotions, and
that's a good thing. Because I feel pretty uncomfortable sitting at
Marchant's table watching "House Hunters."

I'm not sure what's going on with him, but I'm worried I
got in over my head. I mean, let's be honest: I have no experience. The only addict I know is Lizzy's mother, who battled various addictions for years before the long stretch of sobriety she's
enjoying now. Yes, Adam had/has a drinking problem, but I
have a feeling that may be the minor leagues compared to what
Marchant is going through.

Is it withdrawal? He said he'd been to rehab. Would they
really send him home if he wasn't ready? Maybe he left early.
Lizzy's mom used to do that. She also slit her wrists and one
time jumped off the second level balcony inside their house
when her dealer went on an extended visit to France.

Maybe I should go to the hotel.

But I don't want to.

I think I need to get some more data before I consider my
options, so I turn up the volume and try to focus on a house hunt
in Atlanta.

But my mind whirls. I definitely don't get the impression
that he's dangerous. Not to me. But is that foolish? I remember

163

how I met him, inside that atrium at the Wynn. Is he dangerous? Obviously to someone who jumps him when he's drunk.

But to me?

I hear the front door open and turn to see him step into the kitchen doorway. His arms are folded, and the sleeves of his white shirt, rolled up to the elbows, strain around his biceps. He's unbuttoned it at his throat, so I can see a hint of his chest. My gaze drags down his slacks, touching his hips, his legs, even his shoes, before returning to his handsome face.

He's smirking.

Great.

"You haven't honed your powers of discretion, have you, Miss Dalton?"

"I guess not." I'm blushing too boot.

"Do you like the way I look?"

"You know I do."

He takes a few steps closer. I feel sweat prickle between my breasts. "I hope you will excuse me for my rudeness earlier. It won't happen again. But if you want to go to a hotel, I'll understand." He sticks his hands into his pockets, then winces.

"What's wrong?"

He holds his right hand out and frowns at it. "Oh yeah, I burned myself."

"Really? Is there anything I can do?"

He smirks again. "I can handle this one by myself."

I stay seated and feeling slightly silly as he grabs a small Tupperware box from one of the cabinets and slides a pan of sweet potato fries into the oven. Then he walks around the table. He pulls out the chair across from mine and sinks down into it.

I watch as he props his right hand on the table and bends it at the wrist. "Wasn't paying attention," he murmurs as he examines it.

I'm considering whether or not to offer my assistance a second time—he did burn his right hand, after all—when he smiles a little, like he can see just what I'm thinking. "I'm a leftie," he says, "so I'm good."

I nod, prepared for more painful silence. Instead, as he opens the box and pulls out a little square package, he says, "You're one of those goody two-shoes types, huh?"

"What does that mean?"

"You're a goody two-shoes."

"Again: What does that mean? Or, what do *you* mean? If you think about that expression, it doesn't make any sense. Even bad guys wear two shoes." I notice I'm sitting straight up, so I sink back a little, trying not to look offended.

He stretches out the fingers of his right hand, ticking off his points as he gives them. "For one, you don't use dirty language. Unless prompted." He smirks and I know he's referring to our time together in bed.

"And?"

"You came here, to the ranch, a place you probably dislike, because your buddy Carlson was laid up here. Even though you and he weren't on the best of terms."

I nod.

"Because you tried to make a play for him. Am I right?"

"That's not your business."

"So I thought." He looks smug, and I bite my cheek so I don't give anything more away. "Point three: You haven't seen many dicks." My jaw drops as I wonder how the heck he knows that, but he continues. "Four: You jumped into the pool to help a stranger and then conned your way into my ambulance. Plus—" he gives me a sudden, catlike grin— "you've just got that angelic glow thing going."

I drop my head into my hand in mock exasperation. "I am not an angel. Maybe I just seem like one compared to your usual women."

"I have women?"

I humph. "Don't pretend you don't."

"Okay." He holds his left arm out in a surrender gesture. "But I'm not pretending."

"That's ridiculous. Everyone knows you have a bunch of different women."

"Have them?" He shoots a pointed look at me. "As in, they're mine?"

"As in you sleep around. You're a man whore."

He smiles, closed-lipped. "Why can't I just be a whore? Why do you have to distinguish me as a *man*-whore?"

I snort. "So you're a feminist now?"

"Surely you've heard."

"I haven't."

"Well, allow me to enlighten you." He holds up his hand to tick points again. "Women own at this point about thirty-two percent of my company. If any of them get pregnant and want to be pregnant, they get six months maternity leave. They make more money than the men. Plus my dear friend Rachelle, who you may have noticed is a woman, runs the place. A woman who is married to a woman. Also, I think it's kind of hot when women don't shave their legs. So yeah, I'm a fucking feminist." He looks at me, dead pan, and I laugh.

He laughs, too, but as soon as his eyes meet mine again, he looks back down at the wrist he's taping a bandage onto. Like he remembered he's not supposed to talk to me.

But I'm not going to give up. "I took a women's studies course in college. And while a lot of those things are good, I, uh—"

He snorts. "You don't think I'll be invited to any bra burnings?"

"I don't think that's even been a thing since the seventies."

"Maybe not," he concedes. "But what about your feminist credentials?"

Hmmmmm… "I think men should get manicures and pedicures, just the same as women."

He laughs. "You're a trailblazer."

"I have to admit this is more about personal preference than gender equality. Toenails especially. I like a man with well-trimmed toenails."

His shoulders are shaking with his quiet laughter now. As he settles down, his eyes tug up to mine. "I'll be sure to keep my toenails away from you."

I smile, big and slightly silly. "I didn't say *all* men have gross toe-nails. Just that there's something nice about groomed hands and feet." My gaze zips over him, from his neatly tousled hair to his crisp white shirt, to his big hands, spread out on the table. "Have you ever gotten your nails done?"

"Can't say that I have."

"Maybe I could do them for you while I'm here."

Marchant looks slightly helpless. "You could..."

I grin. "Good. It's settled, then. After dinner, you're getting mani-pedi'd."

He chuckles, like he thinks I'm crazy, and gets up without another word, putting the first aid kit back in the cabinet and disappearing in the direction of the front door.

Minutes tick by. HGTV shifts to a show about buying real estate in Hawaii. I keep looking across the kitchen, toward the doorway that adjoins it to the den. Finally, I hear the front door open; hear his footsteps through the den. I smell the burgers and then Marchant comes through the doorway, looking slightly like a sexy waiter in his slacks and white shirt.

"Dinner—" he lowers the tray onto the counter— "is served."

I start to get up, but he waves me down. "What do you like on yours?"

"I'll take everything."

He's quiet as he prepares our burgers, puts some fries on both plates, and opens the refrigerator. "What do you like to drink?"

"Anything is fine. Anything except pineapple juice. Which I doubt you have."

"You're right—I don't. How's lemonade?"

"It's good. Thanks."

A minute later, he's setting my plate and my glass in front of me. He takes the seat across from me again and barely looks my way as he bites into his burger. In fact, I almost feel like he's trying *not* to look at me.

I try my own burger and am surprised by how much I like it. "This is great. I mean...really. What's your secret?"

He looks briefly my way, smirking. "Bison."

"Bison?"

"It's a bison burger."

"Really?" I take another bite, and...I'm not sure how to describe it. I don't eat many burgers. "This is my first time eating bison."

"I'm surprised."

"Why?"

"I'd figure you'd...have a well-rounded palate." He's smiling again now, giving me a hard time.

"You are correct, sir. My tongue is...ah..." I was going to say "well-traveled," but the double entendre was so obvious even I noticed it. I settle on "experienced," which I realize the moment it leaves my mouth isn't any better. Marchant dutifully wiggles his eyebrows, and I roll my eyes. "What you don't know is: Dad's vegan, and that's how we all grew up. So I haven't been eating meat for very long."

He wiggles his eyebrows again, still eating his own burger, and I try not to laugh. "I'm also surprised because it has to be on half the menus of the restaurants in Napa."

"It does?"

He nods seriously. "We're in the middle of a Bison Boom."

"I...haven't heard that."

"Bison. Boom."

"Are you in Napa much?"

He shakes his head.

"But you grew up in California?"

"Yes. I did." He looks weird, and I guess he probably doesn't like to be reminded of growing up, considering his parents are both gone now. I wrack my brain for a topic that might make him feel better. Less lonely. I think I remember Hunter saying something about a sister, so I ask, "Do you have any siblings?"

He sets his burger down, fixing me with a stare that could melt steel. "I have a sister. Riker. She's twenty."

I wait for him to reciprocate, to ask me questions as per the rules of normal conversation, but he just eats quietly, looking maybe slightly pissed off. Or maybe just unhappy. I don't know. I eat a few of my fries, and tell him "these are good, too," but he barely looks my way.

We both watch TV as a couple from North Carolina move to Waikiki, but I'm not really watching. I'm wondering about him and all this hot and cold. It's like he's bipolar. As the show goes off, he finally looks at me again. "You finished?" His eyes are cold and distant.

"Yeah. Thanks again for making it."

He takes out places into the kitchen, then says, "Have a good night. Treat the house like it's yours. I'll see you around nine tomorrow?"

I nod a little, hoping to get a chance to ask him what's on our agenda, but he's gone the next second. I'm alone in Marchant Radcliffe's kitchen. For the first time, I think maybe Lizzy was right.

CHAPTER NINETEEN

Marchant

I'M A FOOL. To think I could handle anyone staying at my house right now.

I go from the kitchen to my room, grabbing a few toiletries I forgot, and then head down the stairs into the basement. It's dark and cool down here, which is usually a good thing. I work out here. But while Suri is here, I'll be sleeping down here, too.

I run my eyes along the rubber-mat floor and think I may not be here as long as I thought. As soon as she gets going with the project, I should take off. Maybe I'll go to my house in Summerlin. Drive back every couple days to check on progress. After the first two weeks, I could go to the cabin. I'd like to get away from Libby. She keeps pushing me to talk about Marissa, and I'm not going to.

I do a hard work out, shower, and drag my camping gear out of a storage closet behind my treadmill. Wearing only boxer-briefs, I slide into a sleeping bag and set my phone's alarm for 7:30, so I can be ready when I meet Rachelle at the front door. I don't want her coming in tomorrow; don't want any chance of Suri Dalton seeing her hand me my Lithium.

I don't need anyone up in my business, especially not someone like her. I've decided the girl's too fucking perfect. Perfect in bed, perfect family, perfect life. If she knew about mine, she'd have nothing but pity for me.

I don't need anybody's pity.

Still, I go to sleep dreaming of sliding back inside of her.

In the dream, I'm fucking Marissa. We're in my bedroom at West Manor—a cavernous place with navy blue walls, floor-to-ceiling bookshelves, a vast oriental rug, a Maplewood canopy bed, and a marble-topped mini bar in spitting distance of said bed.

The room smells like wood polish, old fabric, and Marissa's sweet sex.

Her pussy feels like a glove around my cock. I'm fucking her from behind this afternoon, because she's got a sorority meeting in an hour and she doesn't want me to get my giz all over her pink blouse.

I smack her ass as I pump into her, and she moans. Her honey blonde hair spills around her shoulders—muscular shoulders, because she's on Tulane's swim team.

She cries, "Yes! YES! Marchant, yes!"

Then the ceiling caves in. Flames spring out of nowhere. I can smell the jet fuel burning. And a baby starts to cry.

My eyes flip open and it takes me a minute to figure out where I am: on the floor in my work-out room, panting in my sleeping bag. I'm sweaty. Shaky. But at least I'm not having a nightmare anymore.

I push myself up on my elbows and look at the stairwell. And then I hear it: a crying baby.

What. The. Fuck.

I'm up in seconds, climbing the stairs with a pounding heart—except the more I climb, the fainter the sound is. All the hair on the back of my neck pricks up as I look around the basement. There's no baby here. There's no baby here. Oh, fuck. Is there a baby here?

I dash back down the stairs and look everywhere I can think: behind equipment, in closets, in the pile of dirty clothes in the corner. As I push into the bathroom, I'm shaking so hard I can barely walk.

"Oh fuck. Oh fuck."

I don't want to be crazy.

I can't be crazy.

I'm taking my Lithium.

"Hello?" I shout into the empty room.

The baby cries louder.

I hold my head. I'm imagining these cries.

But it sounds just like a baby.

"Oh God."

I stumble through the room, it tilts around me. I grab the glutes machine and breathe hard.

"Marissa?"

I can't be crazy.

Fuck me. I can't be crazy. Not with Suri Dalton here! I don't want this. I don't want this!

Then I spot the back door. Step toward it. The sound is louder. Louder. Louder. I yank open the door with my heart in my mouth and my lungs frozen in place.

And there are cats. Two cats. I sink to my knees and let a single sob out.

Suri

IT'S A COMFORTABLE bed. Soft sheets. Mattress not too soft or hard. The room has a slight cinnamon smell; cinnamon and cologne. I inhale the scent, roll over on my side to get more comfortable. But that's not the problem. Discomfort is not the reason sleep won't come. It's all the questions in my head.

What books are on the darkened shelves in front of me? What's in the drawers of the nightstand beside the bed? Who's in the backward-facing picture frame on one of the shelves? All I know about Marchant so far is what I've gleaned from his home décor and superficial things, like the types of towels he uses—they're very soft—and the fact that he has a spare bathrobe in a woman's size.

What is with his prickliness? Is it withdrawal, I wonder for the dozenth time? What exactly happened to his parents? I know their plane crashed somewhere in South America, but what were the circumstances? These are things I could ask Lizzy, things I could maybe even look up online, but I won't let myself. If he wants privacy, I'll do my best to respect that.

But I still wonder. What did it feel like to be addicted to drugs? Why does anyone do drugs with a high potential for addiction? In Cross's case, he was taking painkillers for pain—but other than necessity, why would you do that?

Marchant obviously has a reputation, but would he if he wasn't doing drugs? Why didn't Hunter know what was going on? Has he always done drugs, or only recently?

Why do I care?

It's hard to say why. Maybe I don't even know. It's like...every time I'm near him, I feel satisfied. And every time I'm not, I want to be. There's no logic to it. I'm not even entirely sure what I like about being near him.

He's not exactly good company. But he's funny. I like the way he smirks at me. The way he looks when he smiles. I definitely like it when he fucks me.

Thinking about having sex with Marchant makes me feel too hot, so I toss the covers off and flop over on my stomach.

That's when the phone rings.

At least, I think it's a phone ringing. It takes me a moment to see the phone, but then I notice a small, flashing green light on the bookshelf and localize the sound to there. I jump up and grab it, fumbling with the keys to find an "on" button. I press it before I realize I probably shouldn't have.

I hold the phone to my ear, but it's a second before I manage to say, "Hello?" I quickly add: "Radcliffe residence."

There's nothing but breathing on the other end of the line. "Hello?" Is that static, or— No, that's definitely breathing. A million thoughts run through my head, from drug dealers to creditors to card sharks to rival pimps. I feel a rush of protectiveness for Marchant.

"Look, are you in trouble? Do you need something?"

The breathing continues, and I take that as confirmation of my suspicion. It's someone who probably shouldn't be calling here. "Leave us alone," I snap. "Don't call this house again!" I sit the phone on the receiver a little too hard, jarring the bookshelf, and something small falls onto the floor. I scoop it up and carry it over to the window, giving myself permission to check it out since I already knocked it off the shelf. In the moonlight, I blink down at the tiny silver frame. Inside is a grainy image: black and white.

I'm squinting down at it when I hear footsteps.

Marchant

I OPEN THE door quietly. Despite the state I'm in, I will go if she's sleeping. As I turn the knob and nudge the door open with my knee, I pray I find her standing at the window. So vividly am

I imagining the moonlight on her face, when I actually find her kneeling by the window, I'm sure it's a dream.

Then she turns to face me. Moonlight glints off her hair like a crown. Her eyes widen. I step through the door and go to her.

I start gently. My hands on her shoulders. My fingers on her cheeks. My mouth on her mouth. She accepts me readily. Tilts her head back. Helps me lift her t-shirt when my hands delve underneath.

I lead her to the bed and lift her onto it. I spread her legs and stroke the soft skin of her thighs.

"I like these," I tell her, with my thumb inside her shorts. Then I peel them off. She's naked underneath; naked and perfect and soft. Already wet. She arches and moans when I slide my finger into her. When I rub my thumb down her slit, she grabs my shoulders. Her legs lock around my waist.

I'm so fucking hard, I'm worried I might come right now.

With my finger stroking inside her and my thumb teasing her clit, I suck her breasts. I'm so worked up, my cock is crying cum tears. My balls are hard and hot. I feel like I might explode.

She's panting as I lick down her flat, soft belly, lower and lower until I'm flicking my tongue between her lips; between them she's so slick. And salty. I love the way she tastes. I lick her up and down and stroke her till she's pulling my hair and gasping like she just finished a marathon.

"Fuck me, Marchant! Fuck me please!"

That's all it takes. I jerk down my boxer-briefs, palming my heavy balls and rubbing my aching cockhead in her wetness.

I look down at her face. It's twisted almost to the point of pain. "You want me inside you?"

"Jesus, Marchant!"

"Say it."

Her eyes flip open, and they're wild as hell. "Fuck me."

I grab her thighs and rock forward, pushing up into her till I'm buried balls deep. As I start to move, I swear to God I see stars.

Three and a half hours later when I lie back down in my sleeping bag, the workout room is peaceful and silent. So I sleep.

CHAPTER TWENTY

Suri

IS THIS WHAT it's like—waking up after a night of ecstasy? I'm twenty-three, and this is new to me. I feel...radiant. Warm and glowy. A little quieter. A little slower. Soft, like putty. Light as air. Like I might float through the roof and dissipate over the ranch.

I move about his room almost discreetly, taking care to choose my pink dress and green flats, dressing myself piece by piece: slow, as if I have a secret.

I have a secret!

I think I'm addicted to having sex with a pimp.

I giggle.

I grin into the mirror. Drunken grin.

Suri Dalton—sex addict.

That's me.

I had great sex—cha cha cha! I had great sex! I shake my ass.

Another big smile, just for myself, and I slip my earrings into my ears. One half spray of perfume and I'm ready for the day.

I'm halfway to the bedroom door when the phone rings. I pause mid-step as I remember the call from last night. I'm not answering this time. It rings a second time, and then a third. I listen but the house seems quiet. What if it's important? Four times. Five times. I expect an answering machine to kick in, but it doesn't. Six. What's the limit on a landline? Seven? It rings eight times. Wow! Nine times, and I lunge across the room, snatching the cordless phone off its base. It rings a tenth time while I fumble with the "on" button. I don't have a landline at Crestwood Place. This phone is big and weird and—

"Hello?" I say.

Silence hums into my ear.

"Hello?"

My throat feels pinched.

"Hel-lo?"

Cue the goosebumps. Did you ever read an RL Stine book? Too many of them when I was younger. Maybe I should just—

"Hello." The woman's husky voice startles me. So much that I actually flinch.

"Hello?"

"Hello," she says again. My hand around the phone feels colder.

"Hi, you've reached the Radcliffe residence. May I help you?" I sound like a receptionist, but I'm not sure what else to say. It's not my business who calls him. *Not yet*, a tiny voice inside me whispers.

She hesitates. I can feel her hesitation, even though the line is silent.

"Is Marchant in." It's more statement than question somehow—like she doesn't care what I say. Like I'm no one. One in a steady throng of women he probably parades in and out of his house like show hogs.

Her curt voice seems to echo in the silence after. Is there an accent?

"He's not," I tell her. And it's not a lie. He didn't answer, did he? Maybe he's out, or busy. "I'm sorry," I say—and that is a lie. I want her off the phone. But I'm also curious. "Is there something I can tell him for you?"

Another pause. This is probably where she sticks out her lower lip and feels forgotten. *Because she is*, my inner bitch whispers.

"No," she says. "I don't think so. Could you—" Several seconds tick by. When she speaks again, her voice is so quiet I can barely hear her. "Could you tell him that Marissa called?"

"Of course." And, on a whim: "Is he expecting your call?"

"No. He's not." She sounds sad.

I promise to give him the message and press the "off" button, not sure if I actually will.

Marchant

MORNING IS ALWAYS easier than night, but this one dawns especially bright. It's been a long while since I've written anything, but before I even leave my sleeping bag, I write a quick poem about Suri's body with my notepad app. Damn—those fucking curves.

As I shower and dress, I wonder how long till I can tap that shit again. Woman is addictive. The thought reminds me that she thinks I'm an addict. Annoying, yes, but necessary. There's no other way to explain why I'd forgotten we had sex.

I'd much rather her think I'm battling a substance issue than know that my own brain betrayed me. Or, more accurately, my brain was so fucked up, the only way I could get it back to normal was to let a bunch of doctors give me seizures.

I'm not sure why it matters so much, but I want Suri Dalton to think of me as normal. Well, I think as I slide a belt through my slacks—as normal as a pimp can be.

I'm wearing one of my Brionis today, because they're comfortable and fit well. I've got four of them, three Fioravantis, two Huntsmans, two Kitons, and a Caraceni. I've found I'm taken more seriously when I'm dressed for business. Probably because so many people expect to find me dressed for sex.

No. 1, I never fuck my girls, and No. 2, at Love Inc., we're all about the Benjamins.

Before going upstairs, I send a quick text to my money guy to confirm that the transaction to Hawkins went through. I don't need to have that shit hanging above my head. He replies as I climb the stairs. *'Done.'*

Nice.

Despite what a prick he is, I feel a bit of guilt for how I handled things with Hawkins. If I'd been myself, I'd have paid him promptly. Since this was only my second manic episode, I hadn't realized I'd be so reckless with money.

I never expected to have a second manic episode. Fucking naïve.

Still, I'm feeling okay as I sit on my porch. Rachelle arrives in her jogging outfit. She jogs up my steps, and jogs in place as she fishes my pill out of the pocket of her shirt.

"Thanks for bringing this by," I tell her, swallowing it dry.

"No problem, boss man." She looks me over. "You look sharp."

"Thank you."

Her delicate blonde brows wriggle. "You look better than you have in weeks. You get laid or something?"

I try to laugh her off, but I think I come off looking guilty—or even worse, smug.

She snorts. "Good for you."

"You make it sound like I'm a fucking charity case."

She laughs again, her head thrown back. "Now I *know* that is not the case." She gives me a quick roll of her eyes before jogging off. "After tomorrow," she calls over her shoulder, "I'll give them back to you. Sound good?"

"Yeah."

I'm doing okay now. Feeling less head fucked. As I make my way to the kitchen, I'm surprised to find my mood is…pretty damn good. I crank up some Led Zeppelin on my Bose and crack two eggs, planning to whip up breakfast, before I get an even better idea. I'll make something portable, and invite Suri Dalton to the maze with me. Maybe we can have a quick fuck in the bushes.

I grin, and I'm grabbing some fruit out of the pantry when I hear the click of shoes on hardwood, and there she in the doorway between my den and kitchen, looking gorgeous.

I can't help how good I feel. I give her a big, stupid smile.

She grins back at me. "You look nice today."

I look her over, deliberately lingering on her tits. "You look better." I have to fight the urge to yank her dress up and fuck her on the kitchen table. I'm already hard, and I don't try to hide it as I grab a paper bag from a nearby drawer.

"You going out?" she asks me.

"Yeah."

She walks into the kitchen, giving me a great view of her ass, and leans against my counter. With her hair hanging a little past her chin and her pink lips smiling, she looks like a girl someone should love. Which is a fucking weird thing to think.

I rub my head, and she says, "Where ya going?"

"Thought I'd go for a walk." I thought I'd go with her, but now that I see her looking so beautiful and fresh, I'm not so sure. Wasn't I supposed to be keeping this professional?

But it's just a walk, right? It should be pretty hard to ruin the beauty that is Suri Dalton in the course of a twenty-minute walk. And if we fuck? Well, it's not the first time. I'll end this fuck-fest soon. Get some willpower and take off to my house in Summerlin.

Till then… It's been a long time since I took a walk around

the grounds for no reason at all.

I look back over at her to ask if she'll go with me, and find her smiling slightly.

"What?" I ask.

"Oh…nothing." Her smile widens, and she laughs.

"What is it?" I rub my hand over my face. "Do I have a booger?"

"No." Her eyes are twinkling, swear to fucking God.

"Then what?"

"You're packing a lunch for yourself." She's still smiling.

I hold out two apples and a banana, like I'm surrendering a weapon. "You mean this?"

"Yes, that."

I feel a little hot under my collar. "So what? A person's gotta eat."

"I know," she says. "It's cute." And then she giggles. It's a real giggle. Like…I don't know. Something real and nice.

I'm surprised to find it makes me laugh a little, too.

"I was thinking one of them could be for you. You like apples? Or bananas?"

She twirls a piece of her hair, still smiling. I swear to God, this girl is like sunshine. "I like them both. Where are we walking?"

I shrug as I throw the fruit in the paper sack, prompting her to laugh again. "Just around. I like to stretch my legs sometimes."

I squeeze my eyes shut and want to groan, because I sound like an idiot. I screw up my face and pull out my country voice. "Want to throw some stones in the pond? It's real fuuun."

She giggles again. "Sure. I throw a mean stone."

I walk past her, headed toward the 'frige to grab some bottled water. She catches me by the arm and tugs me close to her. I'm still as one of her hands twists around my nape and pulls my face down close to hers. I'm ready to kiss her. Ready to fuck her.

Instead she pulls me even closer and I feel her lips press gently on my forehead.

It's fucking weird, the way it makes me feel. Just…warm in my chest, like someone poured hot water into me.

She looks into my eyes. I must be frowning because she frowns a little, too, then smiles and ruffles my hair. "Don't be so uptight. I just wanted to kiss you. No strings." She pushes me gently away and holds up three fingers. "I swear."

"I know." I give her a small smile and grab the water from the refrigerator, and by the time I've turned around the weirdness of the moment has passed. She grabs an apple out of the paper sack, and I grab the other one, and we leave the sack in the kitchen and head out the front door. I have a memory of walking out of the house with Riker when we were children, armed with bed linens and kitchen utensils. I guess my brain is dredging up strange shit because of Suri's presence in my house. I usually don't let women stay, or even fuck them in my cottage. That's what my room in the main house is— was for.

As we walk toward the pond, she asks, "What are you thinking?"

I shrug. "About the new building."

It's out there in front of us, and the construction crew is already moving this morning. Their big machines beep and buzz as they resurrect the building.

"What about it?" she asks.

"I used to have a room there. Like, my personal room."

"That's cool."

"I mean for sex."

"Okay—still cool, for you, I guess." She gives me an unreadable look.

"I was just wondering if I'm going to rebuild it."

"Are you?"

"I don't know."

We walk a little more, and it's fucking weird, because I

kind of want her to tell me not to. Instead she says, "Did you ever imagine this place would be so successful?"

We sit on some stones by the pond and I tell her about my first few years as a brothel owner, how I started with the Strip location but wanted something more exclusive, something less stereotypical and more high-end. I tell her about how I met each of the girls—and guys. I tell her about the first escorts who worked for me, about the brothel manager who embezzled almost a million dollars from me when I was still green and didn't know to keep a sharp eye on my managers. I even tell her about how my cheesy, framed "first dollar" burned. And she listens. I can tell she listens, and she doesn't judge me even though she's not a fan of sex-for-pay.

About that time Juniper walks by, wearing a black sports bra and hot pink leopard printed tights. She's holding hand weights with little snoopy pictures on the sides. We both laugh.

"Hello," she calls.

"Hello." I smile and Suri waves.

"Whatever works," I say as Juniper passes.

"You know..." Suri sits her apple core on a stone beside her, "when Lizzy said people here were like family, I scoffed at her. But it seems to be true."

I raise my eyebrows. "Are we converting you?"

"Maybe," she says coyly—but she can't keep the grin off her face. She trails her bare foot over the water's edge and looks around. "Who designed your maze?"

"I did actually."

"Really." I nod. "I'm impressed."

I stand up and offer her a hand, which she takes after sliding her sandal back on. I pull her up. "Want to go?"

"Maze walking?" She smiles a little. "I got lost there the other night."

I'm still holding onto her hand. I tuck it closer to me. "If we get lost this time, it'll be because we want to."

We start off over the plush grass, toward the maze, and after a few steps I can tell something is wrong. Our earlier banter and easy conversation is gone. Suri is quiet; her face looks tight, and her hand in mine is still and almost stiff.

I can't think straight knowing something's bothering her, so I give in. "What's wrong?" I ask.

She glances up at me from underneath her long eyelashes. "I was just thinking of before the fire. I was planning on going back to California the next morning."

"Oh yeah?"

She nods. "One of the reasons was you."

My chest aches. I guess because she takes me off guard. "It was?"

She nods.

I've still got her hand. I squeeze it. She squeezes back, proving—as if I needed proof—she's the kindest, most perfect woman alive. Regret oozes through me, dark and messy. "I was an asshole, right? When was it? At the hospital in El Paso?" Everything from around that time is hazy—probably due more to the mania than the ECT that followed—but I definitely remember pressing her against the wall of a hallway. I don't know what I said, but I remember discharging my anger.

I feel ashamed, now.

She doesn't look at me as we step into the maze. Now that we're surrounded by walls of ruthlessly manicured bushes all around us, I fantasize about lying her down face-first on the little pale pebbles, lifting up her skirt and having her here, under the afternoon sky, but the fantasy loses a considerable amount of appeal when I see the tension tugging at her mouth.

I decide in a heartbeat that I want to give her something. Not the truth—that would cost me too much—but something close to it. I want to get as close as I can to honesty with her. I'm not sure why, but I want to.

I squeeze her hand once more and take the plunge: "You

know…you're the only one who knows about my…problem. Besides Rachelle," I say. "And she only knows because they called her. From the…facility."

She looks up at me, wide-eyed, and I push my chicken-shit self forward. "I've been this way since college," I say slowly. And I'm not sure how to follow-up that particular confession without lying big time or telling her what really happened. But I open my mouth and find that words roll out. They're quiet words—hard words. Maybe it's her soft, cool fingers, stroking the back of my hand that makes them easier to say.

"We had a memorial ceremony for my parents on a Sunday. It was spring break Sunday. They died the first Sunday of Spring Break, and this was the last—the day before school started back. My little sister Riker was only twelve. My dad's parents had her. They're the ones who ended up rearing her." I feel a lumpy knot in my throat, because Riker had wanted to live with me—but I couldn't. "I couldn't take her because…" I shake my head and look ahead, at the bush-framed path that turns left in a few more steps.

"I couldn't take her because I was…unfit," I confess. From this point on, I fix my eyes on the path ahead.

"It happened for the first time when I was flying back to school. From Santa Monica to New Orleans. I just…fucking snapped. My parents weren't perfect, but they had always been there." Mom had bouts of mania and also depression, but it was mostly managed, and she and dad had always seemed like they loved each other, and us. "And then one day, I get a call at the frat house—fucking kitchen phone; we had been playing whiffle ball—and some fucking stranger tells me they're dead. Their plane went down in the Ecuadorian Andes. My mom was flying. She crashed into a mountain."

I tug in a deep breath and shock myself by hoarsely adding, "She was bipolar."

CHAPTER TWENTY-ONE

Marchant

SHIT.

I look down at Beauty, and she's nodding gently. She doesn't look shocked or disgusted, so that's good. If anything, her face is softer.

I take a deep breath and let it out slowly; my head is still spinning with the shock of saying this aloud. "My mom was bipolar. She had been going through…a rough patch. And she was flying that day. The flight logs say the weather was clear." I pause because I'm having trouble swallowing. "The plane looked okay, too," I rasp. "What was left of it… I think that's the worst thing," I whisper. "I don't know for sure if it was…her."

"Are you saying you don't know if your mom…crashed on purpose?"

"She tried it before," I choke out. I can't even look at her. It's been so long since I talked about this; I forgot how hard it is.

I drop Suri's hand and fix my eyes on the top of the hedges, where they're trimmed into a perfectly level plane.

Why did I tell her this?

I have only a second to wonder before she wraps her arms around my waist and lays her cheek against my chest.

"Marchant, I'm so sorry."

She looks up at me, and there's so much sympathy in her eyes, the shit is fucking brutal. And suddenly I don't want to see it there. I don't know if I can bear her understanding.

I don't return her hug, but she doesn't let go.

I close my eyes and see Marissa's face, smiling. She's sitting beside me on a white porch swing in front of the sorority house on a humid Sunday afternoon. She grabs my hand and looks into my eyes, still wearing her church dress.

"Marchant, I have something to tell you. But you've gotta promise not to freak, okay?"

I imagine my dad trusted my mom in much the same way Marissa trusted me. And like my mom, I can't be trusted. Because I'm not a normal person. I don't have a right to a relationship.

I step back, prompting Suri to let go of me. "I guess that's why I turned to drugs," I lie. I've been avoiding outright lying until this point, but I don't want her to draw any conclusions.

"I can understand that would be really hard to deal with," Suri says. Then she shakes her head. "Actually I can't. I'm sorry. I want to be honest. I'm not sure how I would ever deal with that."

She holds my gaze with hers, her face twisted into—what? Sympathy or pity? I can't tell. "I don't think I could ever understand, Marchant, but I can see how you would still struggle with it. How it would lead you to…need some kind of escape."

I lock my jaw. Unlock it. What's wrong with her, making excuses for me? Fuck, I'm not even an addict, and she's acting like I'm already on the road to redemption.

"My mom was selfish." That's the only conclusion I can reach. I look down at Suri, wanting her to understand it's not just my mom.

"Someone like that shouldn't have a fucking pilot's license. They shouldn't have children. Or a husband. They shouldn't be allowed to…put other people at risk that way. It's wrong, and trust me, it leads to nothing but badness."

Silence meets my less than eloquent words. Standing there, in front of her, I can hear the beating of my heart. I look down at Suri—perfect Suri. She'll make some guy lucky someday.

"That's really shitty, Marchant. Really, really shitty that you have to go through this."

I grit my teeth because it's time to put an end to this. My dumb confession. "That's how I became…what I am, okay? My family. I had a rough time a while back and started…started using again. I'm really fucking sorry for getting you tied up in all my shit. I think my point is I'm selfish, just like my mom."

And then I disappear around the bend, where I'm alone. The way it should be.

Suri

I GIVE HIM enough time to collect himself. Then I look for him. Which does not go like I thought it would.

After an hour in the maze, I'm lost and tired. Another half hour and I've made it out into the grassy field between the two rows of cottages. It's a sunny day, with warm, white light splashing through the branches of the huge oak trees. The grass looks so green it almost hurts my eyes.

I think about Marchant's story as I walk back to his cottage. I can't imagine what it would be like to lose my parents in that kind of circumstance. It sounds horrible. It definitely gives me more perspective on Marchant, too.

When I get to the cottage, I find the front door locked, so I walk around to the back. There's a note taped to the door.

"I am going to punish you."

I squint down at the handwriting; it's messy and slanted sideways. I glance around once again for Marchant, wondering if he left the note. It had to be him, right? When he doesn't jump out of the bushes dressed in all leather, I try the door and find it unlocked.

"Hello?"

It only takes a minute to confirm I'm alone. I tuck the note into my pocket, intending to ask Marchant about it later, and settle on the couch with a copy of *The New Yorker*.

He walks in the front door not five minutes later. He looks surprised to see me, and he doesn't really meet my eyes. He shoves his hands in his pockets and comes to stand a few feet in front of me. "I'm sorry I left you out there. That was a dick move."

"I walked through the maze a few times. It was really pretty. No big deal."

"Thanks." He makes a face that's kind of an eye roll and rubs a hand over his hair. "Hey, I've gotta do some stuff today. You want to talk to Tom before they start with the interior sheet-rock?

"Sure."

He nods once, then leaves the room. I don't think about the note again until I'm undressing later that afternoon for a shower.

And since I'm thinking of him, I'm not entirely surprised when Marchant slips in after me.

There's no talking. Just his hands, his mouth, and, when I'm spread out on the warm tile floor with water raining down on me, his cock.

I'm on my third orgasm by the time I've acknowledged that I'm wanting something more from him.

He's moving inside me, physically as close as he can get, when he leans down and whispers in my ear: "Why do you do this to me?"

"Why do I do what?" I murmur.

"Why do you make me feel like everything's okay?"

My heart sends warm fuzz through my whole body. "Because it can be okay." I kiss his mouth and lift my hips to take him deeper.

CHAPTER TWENTY-TWO

Marchant

"YOU HELD OUT on me! You cheater!"

I smile smugly at the beautiful woman curled up on the couch beside me. "I'm an English major, Suri. 'Wheel of Fortune' is my thing."

She punches me in the arm—a signature Suri Dalton move. "You acted like you hated it!"

I shrug and grin. "Acted."

She makes a little hmph sound and folds her arm over her breasts, covering up her pert nipples, which stand out underneath my soft, gray night shirt. "I'm gonna get you back for that! Just wait!"

I laugh and thump her on the nose. "You telling me you've got a lot of juicy secrets?"

"Yes," she says insistently. "I'm full of secrets. I'm Pandora's freakin' box!"

"Just so you know, Pandora's Box was full of curses."

She rolls her eyes. "Fine. I'm still full of interesting secrets. Like did you know I can speak three languages?"

"Counting English?"

She nods.

"Spanish," I try.

She glares.

"You know pig latin doesn't count," I joke.

"It's not pig latin."

I purse my lips and look her over, pretending I can see right through her. I nod and put a finger on my chin. "I see..."

"What do you see?"

I grin. "It's sign language."

"What!?" She jumps up and hits me with a pillow, then folds her arms again. My gaze sweeps up her tights-clad legs, over the swell of her breasts, and over her lovely face. I grin wider. "Was I right?"

"Yes you were right! But how? That's like my only hidden talent. My aunt was born deaf. Everyone in my family knows— Gah! Everyone in my *family*." She shakes her head. "I guess someone, sometime has written about my dad's sister Lucy."

I nod, feeling irrationally pleased with myself. "Someone, sometime."

"And you read it," she pouts.

"What can I say?" I shrug. "I'm well-read, baby."

She sits on my lap and frames my face with both of her hands. "How can you be smart? Pimps are supposed to be big, dumb, jocky types."

"I'm jocky!" I stick out my lower lip, and she giggles. I grab a piece of her hair and twist it around my hand, pulling her a little closer to me. "Besides," I whisper in her ear, "I already told you, I'm a mack."

She giggles again. "That's where the term 'mack daddy' comes from, isn't it? That old fourth grade term the boys used when they wanted to be king of the jungle gym?"

I stroke her cheek. "And here I thought you went to private schools."

"I did. But they were dirty little boys."

"You like the dirty boys?" I take her hand and press it against the bulge that's growing under my plaid pajama pants.

She rubs her palm over me—and I'm stretching out on my back, lifting my ass for her as she yanks off my pants. I make quick work of hers and hold her over me while I explore her with my tongue.

She's groaning, her legs collapsing so she sags on top of me, in no time flat.

She's got her arm stretched back underneath her legs so she can work my cock, but her fingers can't reach me.

"Hold on," she says, pulling away from me with a sexy little cry. She climbs on top of my face and takes my cock in her mouth and I can barely think straight.

"Jesus…" She's got this thing she does with her tongue and her lips that's… "Oh, fuck!"

I'm coming in her mouth, worrying about her until she screams my name and I can feel her quiver underneath my tongue.

I lift her off of me, lay her out on the coffee table, and suck her tits for a few minutes till she's writhing again. Then I lift her onto the couch, spread her legs, and plunge inside. She's warm and soft and welcoming. She strokes my face and cries my name, and you know what? I fucking like it. I might even fucking love it.

It's not until we're eating ice cream half an hour later that it hits me like a fucking train.

"I didn't use a condom. Holy fuck." I'm off the couch and on my feet, pacing. "I didn't use a fucking condom! FUCK!"

"Marchant, calm down, it's—"

"You don't understand. You could get pregnant!" I'm breathing hard. There's not enough air in this room. In this house. "Suri, I *always* use a condom. I can't believe it! Fuck me!" I'm covering my face with my hand, feeling the familiar coldness in my hands and feet that harkens a panic attack, when she grabs me by my elbows and says, "STOP! Stop freaking out, Marchant. I'm infertile."

"What?"

Her hazel eyes are wide in a face that suddenly looks break-able. "I can't get pregnant," she says softly. "It's okay." Her shoulders slump. "I've known it for a while. You have nothing to worry about."

She sits down on the couch, folding her legs underneath her.

In the last few days, we've fucked and worked together, and I've never seen her look like she does now. So…vacant.

I go over to the couch and sit on the floor in front of her, surprised by the depth of loss I feel on her behalf.

"I'm sorry." I'm not sure what else to say. But her wide eyes are fixed on my face, so I swallow past the dryness in my throat. "Do you want children?"

"I don't know. I never really got a chance to think about it. Probably, though. I think I'd like to adopt a little girl or boy."

I nod a little. "Well…that's something."

"Something," she says. "Yeah. I guess it is." And, after a moment looking into my eyes: "You don't want kids? Because of…your mother?"

"I don't want an accidental pregnancy," I hedge.

"Well, you're safe with me." She winks, but the smile she gives me is not real.

I wonder what she would think if she knew the truth about my problem.

I tell myself that I'm a fool for wondering.

Suri

I'VE BEEN INVITED to dinner with 'the girls.' In the past four days, Marchant and I kept bumping into Juniper, the British one, and she eventually asked if I'd like to go to fajita night with the Love Inc. ladies who are still hanging around. (Some of them took time off, because there weren't enough cottages for everyone to continue seeing clients).

That was yesterday—the day that turned into the night when I told Marchant about my inability to procreate.

I'm probably being crazy, but I can't shake the feeling that he's been more distant since I told him. Today he was at the cottage most of the day, doing book-keeping stuff, he said, while I sorted through fabrics and colors to create the new look for the almost completely sheet rocked main house interior. I think I've got the floors and paints mostly decided, and I've got a tentative plan for furniture and plants.

I can't wait to share it with Marchant, but that will have to wait until tomorrow. For now, I put on a strappy red dress, silver shoes, and my favorite low-key jewelry, then pull my hair into a casual bun and add lipstick.

When I walk into the living area, I'm hoping to be greeted by a low whistle. Instead, the place is empty. Or I think it is. I'm at the front door, planning to wait for Juniper on the porch, when I hear Marchant's voice from the kitchen.

As soon as I walk in, he ends whatever conversation he was having and drops his phone into his pocket. His eyes find mine, and my sketch-ometer starts going off, because he doesn't even notice I've dressed up. He looks distracted. Unhappy.

"What's wrong?"

He blinks at me like he's just waking up. "Umm…what?"

"You just…you look— Is everything okay?"

"Yeah." He frowns at me. "Where are you going?"

"Fajita night, remember?"

"Oh yeah. Good," he says definitively.

"Glad to be rid of me," I tease.

"I can't hang out tonight. Work stuff," he tells me.

For once, he didn't join me in the shower.

"Everything okay?" I ask.

"Nothing for you to worry about," he says firmly. And there's something about the way he says it... Like no way would it be my business.

It bothers me.

"Okay," I tell him. "See you later tonight."

As I wait on the porch for Juniper, I'm worrying about what will happen when this project is over—worrying about how hard I'm falling for him—when the door opens and he sticks his head outside. "I just wanted to tell you—you look good. Have a good time. They're nice people."

"I know," I smile. "And thanks. Hope you get your work stuff sorted out."

"I hope so too."

There's something odd about the way he says it. I'm still thinking back to it when Juniper and a few of the other girls arrive.

Marchant

MY P.I. CALLED today. So did my finance guy. Apparently someone has been attempting to hack into my money accounts. I assume it's someone working for Rex Hawkins, since I can't think of anyone else who has it out for me.

I spend most of the morning pacing around the cottage, wishing I hadn't re-paid the fucker an extra twenty-five percent on what I owed. Wondering if it was he who sent the text referencing the fire. I know I was late paying him back—and I *did* shoot him in the foot—but shit. How far will the fucker go?

After weeks of reckless mania, worry is a strange, disturbing thing.

I have my money manager report the suspicious activity to some people I know at the FBI, and he comes back with a long list of IP addresses from places like Tokyo, Lima, Paris, and San Diego. Of course he does. My hacker friend isn't going to leave a trace.

I spend some time wishing I could hop on a plane and disappear. Lead my pursuers somewhere far away from here. Trouble is, Love Inc. is an easy target whether I'm here or not. And I guess I'm jumping the gun a little. No one's made a threat. And I really have no idea who is snooping. I'm not exactly low-profile, and a lot of people assume I'm worth a lot more than I really am. Compared to someone like Hunter, I'm a pauper.

I take a long shower and jerk off thinking of Miss Dalton.

After my shower, I get a phone from a withheld number. Normally I'd ignore it, but because of all this other shit I answer, and after a second, I wish I hadn't. Fuck. All I can hear on the other end is heavy breathing.

"Who the fuck is this?"

Click.

I'm worried about Suri, but I find her safe in the main house, talking to Tom about ceiling textures.

I need to calm down.

I have an early afternoon session with Dr. Libby. Three times a week seems excessive, but apparently that's the protocol after a manic episode—especially one that includes an adventure to the bottom of a pool. We talk about Riker, by some strange twist of conversation. She's going to school at UCLA, majoring in environmental science. Libby tries to lead me down the path to my mother—do I remember her being hospitalized for mania?—but I veer the other way. I just don't fucking feel like it.

By the time Suri returns to the cottage around five, I'm like a fucking puppy. I want to feel her. I want to talk to her. And that's when Dave calls back. He doesn't even tell me anything helpful, just confirms that he's got a tracer on my phone line here at the cottage, and the extra security I had Richard bring on are all in place; all doing their jobs.

By the time I get off with Dave, I can hear Suri in the shower. My cock is hard, and I want nothing more than to join her. But I've been fantasizing about confiding in her about my hacker. Ultimately, that's why I don't hop in the shower. This desire to share things with her is clearly against our rules. I just haven't decided what to do about it yet.

Another call from Dave distracts me from making proper conversation with Suri before she heads out. I try to tell myself it's no big deal. I've gotten through most of my life without the woman. I can rough it tonight.

I cook some bacon, eat an apple, and pull a Cuban out of my humidor. Everyone's away tonight. I decide I'll walk the grounds, then maybe the new building. That'll make me feel good.

I walk the maze first. Like the libraries in the main house and the cottages modeled after my childhood home, I made the maze for me. Because I get anxious sometimes. Because even though I've only been full-blown manic twice, I've felt myself start to drift that way more than twice, and when I do, I have to re-focus. To clear my mind and get rid of my anxieties. I like the maze, because I know it. No surprises.

The sun is setting, painting the sky a vibrant indigo. I can already see the first stars blinking their way through the evening sky. For some reason, they make me feel good. You can see lots of stars from my place. You can take a deep breath and smell the grass. When there's a breeze like tonight, you can hear the leaves rustle in the trees. This is my business. This is where I live, where others live, where others come for pleasure. It's not a bad place. And despite how fucking close I came, I didn't ruin it. I didn't burn it to the ground. And even though I gambled away a shit ton of money, I've got more. So I am able to re-build. I might be fucked up—I might be shit for personal relationships—but I'm good at what I do. People like working for me. And I do well enough that even my own fuck-ups can't bring me down.

The more I think about it, the more I think maybe it isn't Hawkins messing with my stuff.

I walk out of the maze nearly an hour later with a weight flung off my shoulders.

As I skirt the pond, I remember being there with Suri, and I have the sudden thought: What if I wasn't bipolar? How would I feel about her then? If I wasn't a danger to her...?

Why am I even wondering? I am. I know I am. Just ask Marissa.

I'll never not be a danger to Suri. Maybe I am good at business, but I'm bad for other people. I like Suri Dalton a lot. I like her not just for the sex. I like her for lots of other things. Like for the Wheel of Fortune. And that's bad. That's really bad.

Still, I'm fighting with myself. I'm remembering how good my mother was with Riker and me—how our childhood was normal and, as best as I can remember, happy. I don't know how the plane went down. I don't know what kind of mood she was in that day. Maybe it *wasn't* mom's fault.

For just a few minutes, I allow myself to remember her. How full her cheeks were when she smiled and how she always smelled like perfumed lotion. I remember the way she used to yank me up off the ground and spin me in a circle while she sang a silly little kid song when I scraped my knee, how one time when I got in trouble for sneaking out of class in high school—planning to kiss Julie Thomas in the janitor's closet—she took the principal to task when he suggested I was a troublemaker.

"He's the president of the debate club!" I remember her exclaiming.

My eyes water a little, because I can still hear the pride and the outrage in her voice.

I'm so overcome in that moment, I sit down on the back steps of the new main house. That's where I am, sometime later, when I hear what sounds like a baby's cry. I look around in the darkness, and I hear something rustle in the brush.

Did the sound come from inside the building, or somewhere nearby in the brush? If cats are inside... Has any of the new hardwood been put down yet? I don't think so, but still. I don't want those damn cats ruining what progress has been made. I look around once more and step through one of the rectangular spaces where the doors will be.

I'm in the lobby area, looking up at the scaffolding of the grand, curved staircase, when I hear a low thump nearby. I look left and right, and left again. Moonlight spills through the huge square spaces where windows will go, but I can't make out what's on the floor.

I flip open my zippo and step slowly closer.

It's a cat. A bloody cat. As my eyes adjust to the firelight, I realize it doesn't have a head.

CHAPTER TWENTY-THREE

Suri

"I'M TELLING YOU, you need to watch it. The first season starts off a wee bit precious, but you'll learn to love the little twerps!" Juniper grins and sticks up one hand in a parting wave as I walk to Marchant's door.

I toss one more glance over my shoulder, and Loveless wags her finger. "Details, woman! Next time I see you, you *will* provide me with details. Even if they're little baby ones."

"We'll see," I laugh, waving. "Thanks for a good night!"

I step into the cottage in a great mood, already looking forward to telling Marchant about my night. I step into the den and sit my purse on a table beside the couch, and he steps out from the kitchen.

I can tell before he opens his mouth that something is wrong. His face looks stony, and his eyes don't meet mine for a long moment. Then he pulls my packed bags from behind his back.

My stomach lurches. "What happened?"

"I'm sorry, Suri, but...you have to go. Tonight."

"What? Why?" My voice is high-pitched.

He shakes his head and strides toward the couch. He sits, then leans over a little and squeezes the bridge of his nose without looking up. His shoulders seem tight. I can feel the tension rolling off him.

"Did something happen?"

When he meets my eyes, his are dark and angry.

"Did I do something?"

"Of course not!"

I jump.

"I'm sorry. I didn't mean to raise my voice. You didn't do anything. It's me. I've had some...things come up. A situation. One that changes things."

"Oh." At first I'm sure he means a woman. Maybe it's Marissa. I bite down on my lip and try to keep my emotions off my face as I look down at my hands. Coming here was a mistake. A terrible mistake. I sink down on the couch beside him. Mostly because my legs feel weak.

His lips touch down on mine the next second. It's a gentle, light kiss with the promise of something deeper—except he pulls away as I start to warm to it.

"Marchant, what happened?"

He shakes his head and looks down at the rug. I'm shocked when, a second later, he says, "Do you remember the guy I got in a fight with at the Wynn?" I nod, and he says, "I think he's been pulling some shit on the ranch. I don't want you here for that."

"What happened?"

He presses his lips together and finally meets my eyes. "I found a headless cat in the main house tonight."

"Oh my *God*!" I'm terrified for him. "That's sick."

He nods grimly. "I'll handle it, but I don't think it's a good idea for you to be here while I do. I think it's probably best if I find someone else to finish the project."

I feel like I've been slapped. "Are you serious? How could you? Without even talking to me? Marchant, I'm your friend if nothing else. You can't expect me just to go because someone's messing with you!"

He laughs roughly. "Of course I can. I asked you to go; you

have to go."

"No I don't. I'm not going. I'm not ready to go. I—I'm finishing the project! If you don't want the burden of keeping me safe and don't trust me to keep myself safe—which you should, I might add—I'll bring in my own security. I have people, I'm sure you know."

Before I'm finished speaking, he's shaking his head. "I can't let you do that. I can't be responsible for something happening to you." I open my mouth, and he puts a finger over it. "I *can't*, Suri. I can't."

"You won't be. I make my own choices!" And something dawns on me. "I've been meaning to tell you something."

His eyebrows rise.

"I answered a call one night where no one said anything. They just breathed. And then another time I got a call from a woman named Marissa. Does that ring a bell?" My voice trails off at the end of the question, because his face has lost its color.

He blinks once, slowly, then puts his left arm out on the couch, as if to steady himself.

"Marchant? Are you okay?"

He doesn't even look my way. Anxiety writhes like a tangle in my stomach as I watch him stand completely still. For like two full minutes.

"Marchant? Who is Marissa?"

His eyes meet mine, and all the heat has gone out of them. "You need to go, Suri. You need to go because I told you to."

"What? No way! I want to know who Marissa is. If you're— if you're leaving me for another woman, I want to—"

His eyes narrow.

Shit! I said 'if you're leaving me' like we're *together*! And we're not together. I'm so stupid!

I dash back to his bedroom with my hand over my face. I'm shaking, embarrassed. So very embarrassed. When did I become such a hanger-on? First with Cross, and now Marchant.

I'm the unwanted woman! The friend or the fuck buddy who thinks she's something more. Where's my pride? Where's my *shame*?

It's right here…

I stumble into the bathroom and lock the door behind me, then I sink down on the edge of the huge tub and let it all out. I sob so hard I can't hear anything. Can't feel anything but my grief over the loss of a man I never even had. I must have some problem. Maybe I just can't stand to be alone. Clearly there's something wrong with me, I'm deficient in some way, I'm pathetic.

The door swings open and Marchant looks down on me, wild-eyed and extremely wide-shouldered in his button-up. He's holding the doorknob. He looks stern. Unhappy.

I shake my head. "I'm really sorry for this. If you want I'll—"

He steps closer. Takes my shoulders. "What I want is for you to strip out of those clothes and get into the shower. What I want is *this*," he says—and then he pulls the straps of my dress down off my shoulders, turns me around, and unzips my dress so that it falls onto the warm stone floor.

He gives me a gentle shove toward the shower, but before I get to it, he grabs me by the wrist and jerks me back. He pulls me to his chest and kisses me hungrily. First my mouth, but he moves south quickly, dropping to his knees as he ravages my breasts and then my belly, moving lower to where I'm wet and waiting for him. He covers my pussy with his hot mouth, and I moan.

"I want you," he pants, "and no one else. But I can't have you…so you'll have to let this…be enough."

I'm ripped in half.

I hate what he's saying.

I love what he's doing.

Either way, I can't stay standing.

My knees give out and he scoops me up and steps into the shower. It's huge—maybe the biggest one I've ever seen—and all he has to do is press a few buttons and it's steaming; heat floods down on us from two huge lamps in the ceiling, followed seconds later by deliciously warm water. He stands me on my feet, quickly strips himself, and takes my face between his two big hands.

"I have to be inside of you. Right now."

I flatten my palms against the muscles of his chest. "Tell me you won't make me leave."

His face twists. "I can't do that, Beauty."

I open my mouth to tell him he can, but I realize that's my problem—dating all the way to Adam. I want things to be the way I want them, and sometimes I don't think enough about how they actually *are*.

"I want you right now," I breathe, and our mouths join while his hand works its way between my legs. He slides a finger inside, and I shake my head.

"No," I say into his neck. I pull away and ease him down onto the warm tile. With water streaming down on us, I crouch with my ass in the air, spread his legs, and suck him into my mouth. I make him come fast and hard, and then I make him come again. I'll respect his wishes if he doesn't want me to stay, but first I'll try to change his mind.

CHAPTER TWENTY-FOUR

Marchant

IT'S THREE A.M., and I'm awake after only two hours' sleep. That's bad. I need a consistent sleep schedule to help deal with the Bipolar. But I can't take my eyes off her. Tomorrow, I'm going to make her leave, if I have to carry her onto the plane myself.

Tonight, I stroke her bare shoulders and I tuck myself around her. I press my face against the warmth of her arm and allow myself to inhale the sweet scent of her skin. Even covered in my soaps, she smells like a woman.

"That feels good," she murmurs, and I freeze.

I contemplate closing my eyes and faking sleep, because I'm not sure I can stand talking to her. More so than even her body, I've become addicted to her words.

"I thought you were asleep," I whisper.

"Not anymore." I can hear the smile in her voice, even though I can't see her face from where I'm lying.

I kiss her arm. "You should go to sleep."

"I will," she says though a yawn. She moves her arm so it's around my back and shoulders, and this time, I close my eyes. It feels good. Her fingers skate over my skin, and I feel her lips touch down atop my head.

"Are you going to tell me?" she whispers.

"Tell you what?" I whisper, too.

She twines her leg around mine. "I want to know why you said what you said in the shower. That you can't 'keep me.'" Silence closes around her words. With my head against her ribs, I can hear her heartbeat.

Ba-boom, ba-boom, ba-boom.

"At first I thought you didn't want me like that," she says quietly, "because I was scared you didn't. But now...now I think maybe I was wrong." Her fingers skate through my hair, bringing out goosebumps on my head. "Will you just tell me? Please? What that makes you want to stay so...far from everyone? Is it...what happened to your parents?"

A wave of ice-cold dread washes through me as I think about what she said earlier. About Marissa. I remember the last time I saw her, lying so still on the pink bedspread inside her dorm room. I remember her voice through the phone down at the jail. I remember the casket—and I know I can't tell Suri. Someone like her...someone so kind and generous; Suri would never understand.

Now that we're as close as we've come to be, I'm not sure how to evade her questions—so I roll over with my back to her.

"Marchant," she whispers. "I have another question. Do you have a baby?"

Suri

REMEMBERING THE PICTURE is what woke me up. The black and white picture I saw that night in the silver picture frame, right before I heard Marchant's footsteps coming down the hall and I dropped it by the curtains. I sneaked out of bed tonight and found it right where I left it—underneath the floor-to-ceiling curtains. One look at the image in the moonlight and I can see it's definitely a baby. Bigger than Lizzy's baby (I recently received a text'd image of something that looked like a lima bean).

I crawl back in bed, and a few minutes later, Marchant rouses. I lie as still as I can while he strokes my body, more gentle than he's ever been when he thought I was awake. I'm starting to get the feeling there's a lot he isn't telling me.

When I murmur, "Do you have a baby?" he goes completely still.

I lean closer to him now, staring at the wide plane of his back. "Is the date on your side a child's birthday?"

He jolts out of bed and whirls to face me.

"What the fuck are you talking about?"

"You left this picture out." I grab the image from underneath my pillow and hold it out.

He snatches it away from me. He looks furious enough to spit. "That's not your business."

"I didn't mean to find it. Marchant, talk to me. I care about you. You can trust me."

He's out of the bed in one easy motion, but he doesn't leave the room. Nor does he put down the picture frame. "You've got to be kidding me? Like, I'm not trying to be an asshole, but don't you think you would have noticed a child running around a brothel?"

"They could be—I don't know, somewhere else." He snorts, and I press, "Do you have a child somewhere?"

"No, I'm not a fucking father, okay?" His chest is heaving. "I don't have a child."

Understanding dawns on me, and I nod slowly.

"You think you know what happened?"

"I think I might," I answer softly.

"What don't you get about fuck buddies? It means all this is irrelevant to you."

I lean forward. "I think we both know that's not true. I'm your friend, Marchant. I care about you."

"You don't know me."

"I know you're a nice guy who's only an asshole when he's using drugs. I know you still grieve for your parents, and I bet you're grieving for this baby, too."

And all at once, his shoulders slump, and he raises a hand to cover up his face. "It was a girl," he whispers. "Marissa was the baby's mother."

My heart twists.

"I haven't talked to her in seven years," he says, rubbing a hand back through his hair. He's pacing now, not even looking over at me as he talks. "I don't know why she would call. There's nothing I can give her. Everything is done."

"What happened?" I whisper.

He lifts his eyes to mine, and they're so bleak, I'm sure I get it this time.

Tears rush into my eyes. I blink quickly. He's had a lot of loss in his life. Too much.

He strides closer to the bed and leans over the footboard. "Don't look at me like that. I don't need your pity."

"I don't pity you." I scoot closer to him, reaching out, but he takes a giant step backward.

"You know why I don't have a daughter, Suri? Because I told her mother to have an abortion."

Marchant

THERE IT IS. The most significant fact of my life—my March 15—spilled at her feet. I watch her face and see the shock in it.

"It was after my parents died. I drank a lot on the plane ride to New Orleans and I thought at first that I was just fucked up over what had happened. But then I got back to my room at West's place, where I lived, and fucked our housekeeper." Suri's eyes widen, and I give her a miserable smile. "She was awful; this black-haired creole woman. Mean as a fucking viper. Nobody liked her, but I wasn't thinking straight. After that, I did a bunch of Hunter's coke and got into a fight with someone at the frat house. Broke an armchair. I was so damn mad—at everything.

"And then Marissa called. She had this church thing in the afternoons, and it was over and she wanted me to come see her. I'm not sure how I got there or even why. We were friends with benefits, not a couple. But I went to the sorority house, and Marissa started talking about scholarships. How she was worried about losing her swimming scholarship. Her mother worked at a gas station and her dad was dead. I remember that part—the part about the scholarship. And I remember her asking something about West Manor. Like could she live there. And I said hell no. it was a guys' place, bunch of keggers and hookers and shit.

"She started crying. Asked me why I was being such an ass. I told her my parents had died. She didn't know that yet—she had a shitty little flip phone that never got good service, and she'd been babysitting cousins in Mississippi for spring break. She hadn't heard.

"She flipped the fuck out. Cried some more. And for some reason, seeing her act like that—over *my* parents— It pissed me off. I started to leave, and that's when she pulled it out. This." I hold up the picture with shaking fingers. I inhale deeply. "That's all I remember from the sorority house. I went out that night and wrecked my Jeep, got booked for DUI, and Hunter bailed me out. It wasn't till later on Monday that I found myself up on the roof of West Manor with a fifth of bourbon and one of Hunter's guns that..." I swallow hard. "I stared down at the street, and I thought about Mom. And I remembered the only time I ever saw her do anything really fucking awful. We were at the mall, and she stepped in front of a truck in the parking lot. And I was old enough to know."

I hold my breath until the emotion swelling up in my throat passes. I dare a glance at Suri. She's staring at me with wide, kind eyes.

I stride closer, leaning over the side of the bed now so our faces are a breath apart. "I'm not a fucking drug addict. I don't even like hard liquor. I'm a beer guy," I sneer.

"But you're bipolar," she says slowly, "like your mom."

I look into Suri's red-rimmed eyes and I can see the sympathy. Or is it pity?

"Because I'm bipolar? You feel sorry for me. Listen to what I told her. Marissa said I told her I fucking hated her. I thought she was a low-class whore who got pregnant on purpose. I told her I'd never support her or the baby. That I'd never even fucking speak to her again. Unless she got an abortion. Her mother was Catholic, Suri. She had no one. She'll tell you I even pulled a few hundreds out of my wallet and threw them in the grass before I left that day." My throat thickens, but I push the words out, because I want to make sure Suri understands. Why I can't be with her. Why she needs to leave the ranch and never, ever look back. Why I'm such an asshole for even kissing her.

"I made her feel like she had to get rid of the baby—and she did." I slump down on the foot of the bed, looking at the curtains. I can see moonlight between them—just a sliver of light in the darkness. "I got a call from her," I say thickly. "It was the seventeenth. A Saturday. And by then I knew shit was going on with me but I was too…fucking scared to go somewhere. Like to a doctor." My voice cracks there. I swallow. Even wait a few beats before continuing, because I'm scared I'll fucking cry.

"Marissa called me… She was crying. She kept saying 'I did it.' But by that time, I was more clear-headed. That's the way it is for me. My mania can last a long time—longer than most people's—but I kinda come in and out." I lean down and put my head in my hands.

"I didn't remember what I'd told her. About the… pregnancy. She didn't believe me of course. She sobbed and she cursed and she told me that she hated me. And when it hit me what she'd done—that when she said 'I did it', she meant she'd…" I shake my head. "I was…fucking ripped apart." My eyes feel wet. I wipe them and keep on staring at the window. But my shoulders start to shake.

"I know people do it when they have to—but those people," I rasp, "it's a choice." I hold my head. "I didn't even remember. I didn't remember telling her to— I don't remember."

I feel her arms around me, feel her cheek against my back, but I don't care. It's not enough. Just like every time I let myself remember this, I feel like I'm falling through an abyss. Snatching at the air, trying to freeze time before I smash into the ground. Trying to freeze time for long enough to make a choice.

But I don't have a choice. I never got one. And I never will.

CHAPTER TWENTY-FIVE

Suri

I'M CRYING, BUT I'm trying to be quiet. This is Marchant's moment—his pain—and I don't want to detract from it by highlighting my own.

But I can't stand to see him like this. I can't stand to see him hurt. I want to help him, but all I can offer is my arms.

I only get to hold him for a moment before he nudges me off and turns around to face me. His eyes are red and wet. His grief has changed his face, so he looks like a stranger. Older.

"Does that answer your question? About my daughter?" His eyes bore into mine.

"Marchant, I'm so, so sor—"

"*No.*" He holds up both hands. "I don't want to hear that shit. Save it for someone else."

He stalks out of the room, leaving me again.

I HOLD MY breath, counting down the hours, but he doesn't return. It seems wrong to go looking for him. Disrespectful of his space. So I don't leave the bed. It's a burden, lying here when I want so much to check on him. Of course, it's nothing compared to what he must be feeling.

After he left, I found the picture, and now it's tucked under my pillow. I didn't have the heart to look at it again.

I wonder how I would react if I made such a huge decision when I was in an altered state. If I'm right about what he was saying, Marchant "woke up" from the haze of his mania, and the deed was done.

Maybe he's right; maybe Marissa made the choice she made because of how he reacted when she told him she was pregnant. But maybe she didn't. Maybe it's something she would have done regardless.

And as for how he acted when he was in a manic state? It's not something he should continue to hang onto. It's not something he can change.

I wish I could tell him that instead of lying here hugging my pillow. I'm staring at the curtains, wondering if he's in the house somewhere or out walking the grounds, when I hear the sound of something shattering. I'm up in a flash, headed toward the bedroom door.

Then the lights go out. Every light in the house. The lights in the bedroom were already out, but the light squeezing it's way under the door vanishes, too, and I just have the sense that it's dark everywhere.

I strain my ears, and I hear footsteps. I think it's Marchant. I hear them stop outside my door. It cracks open—my eyes have adjusted so I can see the vague shape of the door as it moves, but nothing behind it.

"Marchant?"

I hear a woman's laugh, and my blood runs cold.

I lunge in the general direction of the bed, thinking I could hide under it, maybe, but scary woman knows. She cries out and I hear her run toward me. Something sharp bites my neck where it meets my shoulder. The pain blossoms as I fall to my knees. I press my hand against the spot that hurts and come away with wet fingers.

"Holy shit!" My heart is pounding as I stand back up on shaky legs. It's too dark. I can't see! I'm panicking. I turn a circle, shielding myself with my arms like I do in Tai Chi, and I'm grabbed from behind.

"Die, bitch!"

I feel another slashing sting across my cheek, and strong hands throw me to the floor. I'm kicked just once before I scream.

At that instant the lights come on. Through the agonizing pain I catch a glimpse of a tall woman with long hair. The window breaks—she jumped through the window, like some kind of supervillan!—and the next moment Marchant bursts into the room.

I cry out in pain as he lifts me onto the bed.

"Suri, what happened? Talk to me, please, baby!"

"Where is she?" I croak.

Moonlight streams in through the broken window. Marchant dashes to the window. I'm curling into a ball, panting through the terrible stabbing in my ribs, when he yells out the broken window, "Son of a bitch!" He lunges for the cordless landline, and as I hear him barking orders to security, I whisper: "Wasn't a...son."

Marchant

AS SOON AS I turn on the lights and realize Suri is okay, I try to dial my terror back a notch. She's got what looks like a knife slash on her neck, another on her cheek, and the doctors I called out to the house are pretty sure she has some bruised ribs. But she's okay.

The cops are on their way, along with an FBI guy, and Dr. Ronland is coming back in a few hours with a portable X-ray machine. Until then, I'm trying hard to keep my shit together.

To do this, I can't talk to her. Can't even stand too close to her. If I do, I'll crack. I can fucking feel it.

After she's swallowed pain pills and I get her comfortable in my bed, I pace the hall that adjoins my bedroom to the den, shifting my attention from the broken window in the foyer to the small, still figure under the blankets on my bed.

How did this happen?

Regardless, it won't happen again.

I've called in even more security—there are now almost two dozen guards patrolling the ranch—and I've taken the liberty of contacting Lizzy, who said she could arrange to have Suri's plane in Vegas in just a few hours. I'm taking no more chances. I don't care if she hates me for sending her away.

That thought makes me sweat. I lean against the doorway of the bedroom, working my jaw until it pops. Who attacked Suri— and why? If she was coming for me, why did she call Suri a bitch? Suri said she might have detected an accent, but she wasn't sure, because her attacker said so little. Could it have been Marissa's Cajun accent?

Marissa is a suspect, no matter how little I want her to be. Dave is finding out everything he can about her right now. I've warned our head of security to watch for a blonde woman, and I plan to tell the police the same thing. I have no idea what Marissa might look like now, but Dave should know soon. He's a good P.I., and I trust him.

I'm feeling lightheaded, so I breathe into the crook of my arm. But the guilt I'm trying so hard to keep at bay breaks through and almost drowns me.

I shouldn't have left her in here earlier.

Oh, God.

What would I do if something worse had happened?

I watch her pretty, sleeping face through bleary eyes, and suddenly I just can't stay away. I climb into the bed as gently as I can and lie beside her.

I shut my eyes and feel the weight of the last twelve hours. I'm embarrassed. Ashamed. That I broke down in front of Suri. That I left her here alone. I can't seem to stay in one place to save my fucking life. I'm good at running away. Maybe because I've never had anyone to stick around for.

Or because I shouldn't.

I've got to come to terms with this. As soon as she's feeling well enough to travel, Suri will be leaving. It might suck for me, but it's the only right choice.

Still…I watch her chest as it rises and falls. I scoot a little closer, even though I know I probably shouldn't.

I don't want to disturb her, so I wrap my arm around her pillows—and pause when my fingers bump something cool. I come out with the ultrasound image.

She put this under her pillow? I wonder why.

My chest aches as I look at the grainy, black and white image. I don't know why I keep it in my room. I guess for the same reason I got the tattoo. I forget so many things… Wouldn't it be wrong to let myself forget this one?

My eyes sting, and I sink my teeth into the inside of my cheek. Doesn't work. Shit leaks all over my face regardless.

I cover up with my arm, feeling glad no one's around to see me weeping.

Suri

MARCHANT MUST BE really tired. He slept through the police officers' drop-by, as well as a visit from the window repairwoman. Combined, both visits lasted less than two hours, but still, I'm surprised he didn't wake up.

Now that I've taken some painkillers and figured out how to move without jarring the left side of my chest too much, I'm feeling a little more human. It still hurts to climb back into bed, but it's where I want to be.

I was asleep when Marchant climbed into bed beside me, and before that, the house was filled with his security team and the doctors who stitched my neck up and put a big sticker on my cheek. Which means we haven't had a single moment alone since he told me…what he told me in the middle of the night.

I watch his face carefully as I settle on my pillows. When he doesn't move, I scoot a little closer. There's a big, annoying pillow between the two of us, so I move it. I take my time sidling closer and closer to him

As I press myself against him, I long to feel the safety of his arms around me. Then he stirs a little, and his arm loops over me. It hurts my chest a little, but it feels good, too.

On impulse, I scoot even closer, pressing my cheek against his lightly bearded one.

"Oh, Marchant…"

I shut my eyes and kiss him lightly on the neck. Very softly, I whisper, "Please be nicer to yourself. You're a good guy."

Tears glitter in my eyes as I think about leaving. After what happened this morning, I know there's no way he'll let me stay.

Just like I know that when I go, I won't be coming back.

I watch his right hand, lying on his chest. It rises and falls evenly, which means he's still asleep. I take the risk of wrapping my arm around his hips.

It's hard to think about the meaning of the tattoo under my arm. I picture a younger Marchant, confused about what's happening to him and anguished over what he perceives to be an unforgivable mistake.

"Please be easier on yourself," I whisper to his sleeping face. "I can't stand to leave you like this."

I think of all the time we've spent together in the days I've been here. He hasn't always been the perfect guy, but we've had fun. More than I expected, that's for sure. More than I've ever had with…well, with most people.

How funny that is. I wouldn't have thought. But as I look at his closed eyes and his bearded cheeks, I feel like I know him. I feel like he's mine.

The realization makes me flush. I feel raw and off balance, elated and sick. And it dawns on me. "I think I love you."

My sleeping beau opens his eyes.

CHAPTER TWENTY-SIX

Marchant

IN MY DREAM, Suri tells me she loves me. I'm lying in a cloud, but I can feel her wrapped around me. It's amazing.

And then something jabs me in the inner thigh. A knee? A foot?

"Marchant," someone hisses loudly, "wake up. I miss you."

And it's weird, because that sounds like Suri, too.

How many Suris are there in heaven?

I crack my eyes open, and I see only one. She has a bandage on her cheek, and— Okay, not dreaming. I remember what happened earlier today and sit straight up, feeling like an idiot for nodding off.

I reach for her face before I remember it's not appropriate anymore and draw back my hand. "You okay?"

She nods, and I realize I might as well have touched her. She's pretty much wrapped around me, and she's smiling at me sweetly. "I just missed you. Sorry I kinda woke you up."

Heat suffuses me. My eyes ache with unshed tears— because I remember dreaming that she said she loved me.

She runs a tickling finger across my forehead, then proceeds to trace the top of my ear. "You sleep okay?"

I swallow. Nod. I clench my jaw and drag a shaky breath in

through my nose.

"I'm glad you climbed in bed with me," she says.

And for some reason, that simple statement is what does it. The first sob sneaks out with some punch, and I roll over on my side, away from her.

I cover my head with my arms. I'm such a fucking freak— but my self-loathing doesn't stop the tears.

I want her and I can't have her. Hurts so fucking bad. Is so confusing. I told her why I stay away from everyone and she's lying here in bed with me, as if she didn't hear any of it.

A second later, she's wrapped around me from behind, pressing her cheek against my back. She's rubbing my arm. Stroking my hair. She's whispering my name.

"Marchant...it's okay. It's okay. I'm here. Everything's okay. You're okay..."

What I am is helpless. I can't stop this shit from pouring out of me. It's like every negative emotion I've held in since college is in my eyes.

Even when I regain some control, my body jerks in weird, uncontrollable shudders. My breaths sound loud and wet and messy.

"Like a fucking toddler," I mutter—although I can't even really manage that. My voice sounds broken.

"No you're not a toddler." She kisses my neck. "You're just a person, Marchant. Like every other person."

She's stroking my back as she says this, and I think I know what she's trying to impart. I shake my head.

She snuggles in a little closer and begins to stroke my back. "I want to tell you something. I want to tell you something no one knows, and it's about Adam."

My muscles tighten a little at the mention of her ex, proving I'm a pigheaded idiot for her.

"Most people think Adam and I broke up because we realized we weren't right for one another. Really? We broke up because Adam has a drinking problem, and when drunk, he liked to call me names. Not fun, sexy names; real names. And one night, when we were in the pool behind my house, Adam was drunk and he grabbed my wrist and I fell and knocked a tooth out." Her hand comes around me and grabs my hand, and she brings it to her mouth.

"You feel this tooth? It's fake."

I get the nerve to turn around and face her fully. She's got a pillow propped under her ribs, and I feel like shit knowing that I'm the reason why. Someone attacked her in my home, and I wasn't around to protect her because I was in the basement, feeling sorry for myself.

It's inexcusable.

Her hand comes under my chin, and I raise my eyes to hers. "Marchant, I'm okay," she murmurs.

"I'm that obvious?"

"Not always." She smiles a little, and I remember what we're talking about. Her ex, Adam. Abusive Adam. Someone needs to kick his fucking ass.

"You're obvious now, too. You think you need to beat him up? No. You don't." She runs a slender finger over my eyebrows; it feels so good I calm a little. "I'm done with Adam. I'm telling you this because, Marchant... Adam is not bipolar. He's got two living parents—both great people. But he wasn't good for me."

"What do you think that proves?"

"What I'm trying to say is that you have to take life on a person-by-person basis. Everyone is different. Lizzy's mother has a drug problem. She's been diagnosed bipolar before, although I don't think she is. But if she was? Are you just like her? Larry Flint is bipolar, I've heard. I don't think Saddam Hussein was. It doesn't define you. Surely you don't think it does?"

"It means I can't be trusted." I rub my head. "I do impulsive, stupid things that ruin lives."

"Okay. Question: How many manic episodes have you had?"

I shrug, feeling self-conscious. "Mine last a while, and I've had two I think."

"Two's not a lot. Could you be trusted in the interim?"

"I like to gamble sometimes," I confess.

"Do you gamble excessively?"

"I get myself into a place I don't like sometimes. But I also win a lot." I arch a brow.

"That sounds normal enough."

I shake my head. "I'm not normal. I'll never be normal."

"What if I don't want you normal?"

Stillness settles over me like a warm blanket. "What do you mean?"

"I mean I…want you, Marchant."

"You want me how?" I rasp. "I want you like, I want you."

"For sex," I murmur.

"More you."

My mouth moves on its own. I swear it does. Because I say, "I want you, too."

Suri

WE SPEND THE next few hours in bed, cocooned in blankets and pillows. I'm caught up in a weird combination of feelings. I'm elated that Marchant said he wants me, too. I can't get enough of touching him, talking to him. And yet, I'm kind of scared. The police officer I talked to didn't seem to take the break-in very seriously and the FBI agent won't be here for a few more hours still, but Marchant's security team is on it; working in conjunction with state law enforcement. I feel safe now, with Marchant right by me, but sometimes when I close my eyes, I feel like I'm still standing at the foot of the bed, waiting to see what will come at me next.

In between kissing me—*everywhere*—Marchant keeps in touch with the security people.

"What are they saying?" I ask after coming out of the bathroom. I heard him on the phone while I was in there, showering.

He turns to me with a weird, expressionless face. "I think they caught the person who attacked you."

"You're kidding. Who?"

His lips pinch. "One of the ex-SEALS on the team spotted Marissa at a gas station a few miles away. She's wearing her hair long. When an officer received the tip from my guy and found a reason to pull her over, she started crying, then claimed that she had come to find me as part of her AA steps."

He just sits there, staring at me without moving or even breathing, and the first thing I feel is a rush of sympathy for him.

"Marchant—God. That's crazy. Did they arrest her?"

He nods once. "Turns out she was driving on a suspended license."

"Oh." So that's it. "Wow. That's so weird. That she would show up again after all this time."

"I don't get it."

"What do you mean?"

"Why she would do this. Like you said, after so much time."

I look up at his face. It's solemn, guilt-ridden, so I grab his hand and squeeze. "You didn't do this, Marchant. Marissa did. And I'm okay."

"You have bruised ribs and stitches." He's up now, off the bed and pacing. "That is not okay."

"It's not your fault," I repeat.

He stops mid-step. "Suri—can't you see? This is *never* going to end. As long as I'm me, this shit will happen. And anyone who's with me will get caught in the crossfire, whether it's dangerous exes or debtors or me."

I close the space between us and grab his neck, wrapping both my arms around him and pulling him down close. "I'll take your crossfire, any day," I say into his collar. "It's better than a day without you. Marchant—" I pull away and look into his eyes— "I don't want to go. I want to stay here, and finish up the job, and finish this with you. I want to figure out where it might be going. And please don't tell me I don't know what I'm getting into. I can make my own choices, and I choose you."

He stares at me again—that long, hard stare that gets the butterflies fired up in my stomach. After a few thunderous heartbeats, he stuns me with a little smile. "So call Lizzy."

And that's how I see the text—the one that says: "We're on our way. Hunt n me, and Cross + Merri, too. Suri...I'm wearing white! We want to do this now! This week! In Vegas!"

I squeal and hold the phone up so Marchant can read the text. His eyes widen, and he says, "Well, hot damn."

"Will you be my date to the wedding?"

He pulls me down onto the mattress with him. He tucks a strand of hair behind my ear and whispers, in a husky voice that sends chills racing over my skin: "If you'll have me, Suri Dalton."

"I will have you." I grin wickedly. "If I lie still so I don't hurt my chest, can I have you right now?"

"Fuck yes."

I'm so busy pulling him down over me, I don't notice the shadow outside the window.

ABOUT ELLA

ELLA JAMES IS A Colorado author who writes teen and adult romance. She is happily married to a man who knows how to wield a red pen, and together they are raising two children under three who will probably grow up believing everyone's parents go to war over the placement of a comma.

Ella's books have been listed on numerous Amazon bestseller lists; two were listed among Amazon's Top 100 Young Adult Ebooks of 2012.

To find out more about Ella's projects and get dates on upcoming releases, find her on Facebook at *facebook.com/ellajamesauthorpage* and follow her blog, *www.ellajamesbooks.com*. Questions or comments? Tweet her at *author_ellaj* or e-mail her at *ella_f_james@ymail.com*

OTHER TITLES BY ELLA JAMES

STAINED SERIES
Stained
Stolen
Chosen
Exalted

HERE TRILOGY
Here
Trapped

LOVE, INC. SERIES
Selling Scarlett
Taming Cross
Unmaking Marchant